Praise for
Off The Well-Lit Path

"Holm beautifully combines two typically incongruent fictional genres: a gripping, action-packed novel and an emotionally astute drama. His writing is poetically austere at times, invoking the hard-boiled prose of Cormac McCarthy. And the surfeit of action the book delivers unfolds in captivating language, the violence terrifyingly real, the danger sickeningly ubiquitous … A thrilling and moving story of love and desperation … A memorable literary experience."

— *Kirkus Reviews*

"Danger, fear, and violence come shockingly to life in this searing tale of modern Mexico. From deserted desert highways to crowded city streets, mayhem is ever present as marauding gangs ply their contemptible trade. Police are either too corrupt or too powerless to stop the rampant bedlam as citizens and tourists alike become prey for criminals immersed in a culture of brutality. The environment Holm depicts asks no quarter and gives none. It is a realistically frightening world guaranteed to stay with you long after the last page has been turned."

— Joe Kilgore *US Review of Books*
Recommended

"Bare bones but rhythmic in its flow … *Off The Well-Lit Path* is a thriller that's focused on vengeance and the dark side of humanity … Captivating and ultimately satisfying."

— JOHN M. MURRAY
FOREWORD REVIEWS
FIVE-STAR REVIEW

"*Off The Well-Lit Path* is a spare, violent literary thriller that delivers an intense and utterly absorbing reading experience … Holm has delivered a bruising but outstanding thriller about how far a father will go for love."

— *BLUE INK REVIEW*
STARRED REVIEW

M.S. Holm

OFF THE WELL-LIT PATH

M. S. Holm is the author of five previous books. Among his honors are the Moonbeam Winner Award and the ForeWord Book-of-the-Year Finalist.

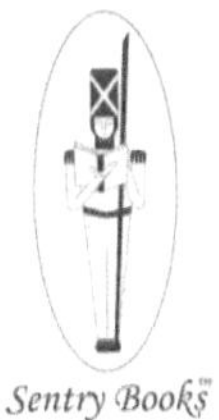

Also by M. S. Holm

The Arborist

How Mohammed Saved Miss Liberty

Cuando Tu Camión Escolar Se Va a México

The Poor Gringo Guide to Mexican Cooking

Driller

OFF THE WELL-LIT PATH

M.S. HOLM

Sentry Books™

Great West Publishing
USA

Sentry Books

An imprint of Great West Publishing

Off The Well-Lit Path

For information about this title or to order other books and/or electronic media, contact the publisher:
www.sentrybooks.com
sales@sentrybooks.com

Library of Congress Control Number: 2018958060

Publisher's Cataloging-in-Publication data

Holm, M. S.
Off The Well-Lit Path / by M. S. Holm — First Edition
Description: Tucson, AZ: Sentry Books, an imprint of Great West Publishing, 2019.
Identifiers: LCCN: 2018958060 | ISBN: 978-0-9974553-8-0 (pbk.) | 978-0-9974553-7-3 (ebook)
Subjects: LCSH Americans — Mexico — Fiction. | Cartels — Fiction. | Crime — Mexico — Fiction. | Criminals — Fiction. | Kidnapping — Fiction. | Fathers and daughters — Fiction. | Suspense fiction. | BISAC FICTION / Crime | FICTION / Westerns
Classification: LCC PS3619.A992 O44 2019 | DDC 813.6–dc23

ISBN: 978-0-9974553-8-0

Printed in the United States of America

Map of Sinaloa by Sarah Garibaldi
Lineup Photograph: eldebate.com
Cover: 1106 Design

This book is dedicated to

FRANCIS HARVEY SAYLES Jr.

Organized crime as defined by Mexico's legal code, approved February 1994: "three or more persons organized under rules of discipline and hierarchy in order to commit, in a violent and repeated way or with the purpose of profit, any of the crimes legally defined."

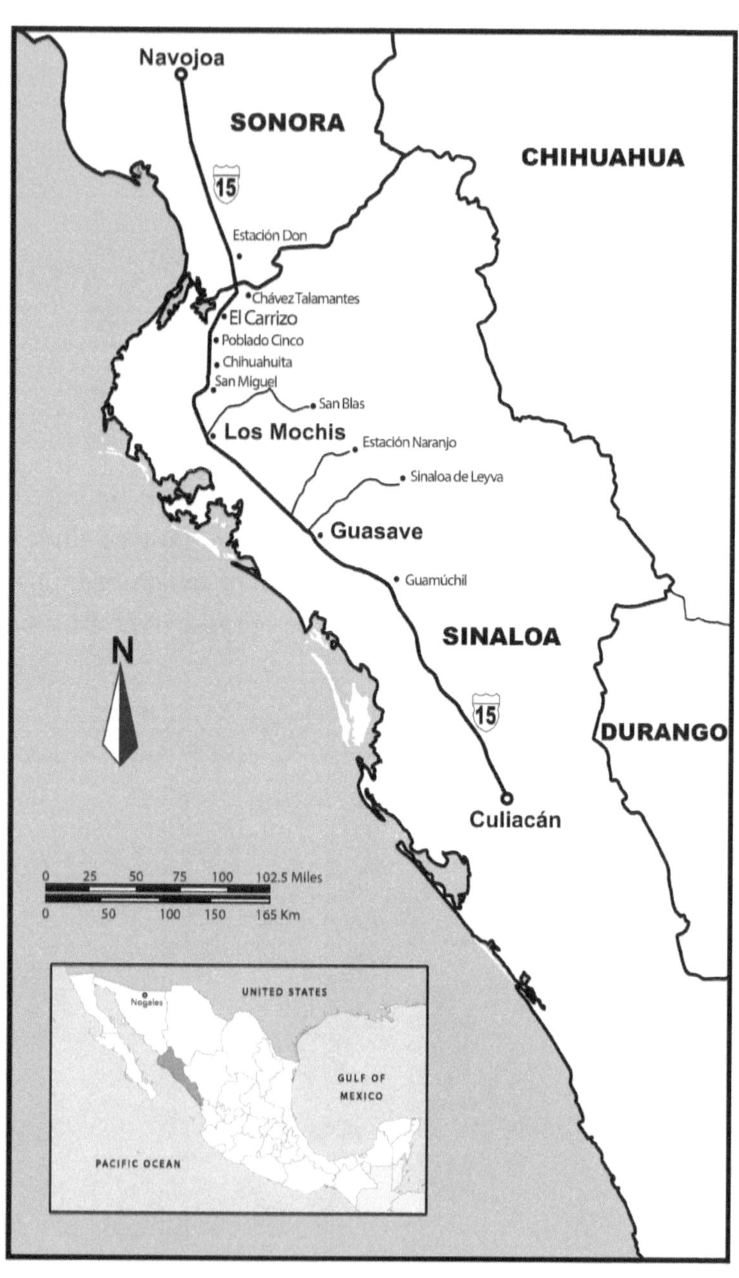

Navojoa
SONORA
CHIHUAHUA
15
Estación Don
Chávez Talamantes
El Carrizo
Poblado Cinco
Chihuahuita
San Miguel
San Blas
Los Mochis
Estación Naranjo
Sinaloa de Leyva
Guasave
Guamúchil
SINALOA
15
DURANGO
Culiacán
N
0 25 50 75 100 102.5 Miles
0 50 100 150 165 Km
Nogales
UNITED STATES
GULF OF MEXICO
PACIFIC OCEAN

1

It's a rush, running wide open, the blast of wind on our faces before the windows roll up and our masks come down. The gun oil smell. Everything racing, no one talking, just watching as we close, knowing it could go wrong but knowing it won't because we've done it a hundred times and we're still alive and who's going to stop us and who's more afraid of dying? I watch their gringo faces go pale — the best moment and always the same — when they realize it's too late to save themselves. Their scared eyes. The sick looks. Then we're on them like roaches. How the Indians used to do it before they became gringos, before the roads were paved, finding the solitary wagon, circling, whooping and wild, taking trophies. There's no better feeling than belonging to such a party, running with the men. It's a rush, like I said.

RUGG NEVER SAW WHERE they took to the highway. Stealth perfected. Empty asphalt in his rearview. When the white Cheyenne appeared alongside, it ran close enough for him to glimpse his reflection in the polarized glass — how he was seen, his wonder and advertence. He backed off the accelerator to let it pass. Then the Cheyenne's windows came down, their masked faces daylit. No badges, no khaki. One of them waved a pistol.

"Rose," he said.

Her bare feet rode the dash. Her ears wired to a world he almost heard.

"Rose."

"What?"

"Get the passports. Your shoes."

The Cheyenne clung to the pickup, one shadow running. Their shouts heard through the glass. Rugg did not look at them.

"Who are they, Dad?"

"Some men. Get the passports."

"Where?"

The road straight, the shoulder dropping steeply to a range fence. Beyond it the desert lay flat. The scrub thick and without dwelling. He considered their chances to outrun them should the pickup not roll from a shot tire, should the masked men not shoot the windows. Small chance.

"In the bag, Rose. Put on your shoes." The cockpit calm kept in his voice.

He coasted, no brakes, not wanting a sudden stop to be mistaken for cleverness or stupidity. The shoulder not wide enough for the truck to fully side the road. When the Cheyenne cornered the front bumper, Rugg braked hard to avoid a collision.

The four doors opened. Quick like flies, they swarmed the pickup. One of the gavilleros pulled at the driver's door. He gestured for Rugg to unlock it. "¡Ábrelo!" he ordered. A second masked man rapped on Rose's window with his weapon.

"Dad!"

Rugg unlocked the doors.

Her bare feet the last thing he saw before they pulled him out, the truck motor still idling. They manhandled him to the highway centerline, where they released him and took aim. Rugg glimpsed the arrival of other vehicles, the occupants getting down, their faces also masked. He raised his hands and lowered his gaze. He knew to do this.

"Please! Please!" cried Rose.

Don't, Rugg thought. Don't speak.

"Please! Leave us alone!"

The small gavillero who approached him wore flashy sneakers and walked with a limp. His pant waist showed a pistol with a silver grip. He ducked into Rugg's downturned gaze, his mask a sock hat with scissor-cut holes. He winked through an eyehole before he patted Rugg's pockets, lifting his wallet so cleanly Rugg wasn't sure it was taken until he saw it held. His watch and ring not taken.

Rose began to scream. "Stop this! I want my dad!"

A man's voice ordered her to shut up. "Zip it or we kill you both." The voice graveled, the English clean. Rugg believed the man's words, and he did not believe what most men said.

Rose began to cry.

Across the blacktop Rugg's shadow cast to the highway's edge. He had told her about the passports, the shoes. He had not told her about silence. So much not told. Rugg's life clocked to a standstill. He saw himself distantly, a stranger sharing the two-legged likeness of men. He remembered a rancher from years back who had told him that when a horse saw another horse, it did not see a horse. What it saw was a stranger made like a horse. So Rugg saw himself.

He heard a large truck approach, the harmonic whine of its weighted tires. He heard the downshift and the chatter of a Jake brake, and then he heard the big diesel idle at a cautionary distance.

The gavilleros stood. Rugg watched their stilled shadows on the blacktop. He glimpsed the Cheyenne, no plate on it.

"Él se queda," ordered the graveled voice.

They grabbed him by the arms and pulled him off the highway.

"Dad!"

When Rugg saw the embankment, he wrested himself from them and turned to where the graveled voice had spoken. "Take me," he shouted. "I'm worth it."

The boss stood taller than the others. No mask covered his face. His silver hair short-cropped. Rugg did not try to see more.

"Worth what, my friend?"

"More money," said Rugg. "Less trouble. Take me."

The boss studied him. "But you are not as pretty. Eres un gringo feo."

The men laughed.

Rugg shook his head. "No. It's a good trade."

"I will let you run," the boss said. "She will not see. That is a good trade."

"She is all I have."

"Then you have nothing, my friend."

No reprieve in his voice. A stone sooner turned cold in hell. Rugg looked at him. His face handsome to a degree beyond good looks or grooming. Cruelty absent. Misdeeds unmarked. A child's frank gaze. Why he wore no mask. Why none needed.

"Please," Rugg said, the word saved for this moment.

The boss smiled. "We call it the *ley fuga*. There is no good translation. It is a law of luck." He chinned toward the desert at a distant point where the land met the sky. "You must run fast."

The men retook Rugg. "Wait!" he said. "Wait!"

He pushed them. The men agile and wiry. One of them swung his weapon and broke Rugg's jaw. He knew it was broken when he called her name, the sound flung raw from his mouth. They dragged him down the embankment. He heard Rose scream. He thrashed and kicked.

"Daaad!"

The highway fence strung with livestock mesh topped with barbed wire held to T-posts. They muscled Rugg over the top.

He landed torn and twisted. When he stood, he stared slack-jawed.

"¡Corre!" they shouted. They pointed to where Rugg should run into the desert.

The rumble of the diesel truck idled in Rugg's head. He heard car doors slam. He saw his pickup retake the road, tires spitting gravel. He saw the white Cheyenne in pursuit. He did not see Rose.

"¡Corre!"

A weapon clicked. Not here, Rugg thought. His last memory of her not bled to this spot.

The one who had broken his jaw climbed the wire fence. He shoved Rugg. "¡Corre!"

Rugg stood.

"¡Corre, hijo de tu puta madre!"

When the man tried to kick Rugg, Rugg knocked him to the ground with a punch. Two gavilleros watched from behind the fence, their weapons shouldered. "Órale," one of them said.

The kicker got to his feet. A rib-knit, three-hole balaclava covered his face. He touched the mask where Rugg had struck him. Rugg saw the man's drugged eyes, his bad teeth. A large knife sheathed on his belt.

"Roon, greengo," he slurred.

His weapon a pistol-caliber carbine with a short box magazine. The stock worn, the bluing gone from the barrel. Rugg saw the muzzle soiled from when the man had fallen to the ground from the punch.

"Roon, greengo." He raised the carbine and pointed it.

Rugg measured the man's narcotized stare and the way he stood with his feet together, his left shoulder dropped in a southpaw stance. The first round likely to go right, he guessed. The muzzle likely to blow dust. Then what, he could not guess.

The fenceline cleared of scrub where range cattle had trampled and grazed. The men behind the wire spectated shoulder to shoulder. "Déjate de pendejadas," one of them told the drugged gavillero. "Mátalo ya."

On the highway their ride waited, its doors open. Rugg heard the air brakes release on the big diesel. He heard the truck's slow advance. He did not look at it, his eyes fixed on the gavillero's weapon, how his finger held the trigger. When he saw the knuckle lines disappear, Rugg sprang left along the fence. He knew he had cleared the shot when he heard it, when he felt nothing — no stab, no bludgeon — his breath not sucked from a gaping hole, light's beauty not eclipsed. He rose and scrambled up the fenceline, their shouts and gunmetal clatter a muted babel to him, his world a paper-thin sphere across which he must hurry or fall through. At the first scrub opening he broke from the fence and ran flat and shadow-clung, like something four-footed scurrying to its hole. Fear contracted. Life shrunk to a final moment. He cut a zigzagged path, threading the brush gaps to put cover behind him. No sharpshooter rose to preeminence among them, their wild gunning set upon his white shirt, the fusillade snapping thornscrub limbs.

The desert without gully or outcrop. A vanished sea had left Rugg no concealment beyond the holes of long dead foraminifera, their benthic shells crunching under his feet. He ran with his mouth blooded and agape, as though in astonishment at a newly broken world, one where masked marauders set a man free so that they might shoot him in the back. He weaved and dodged, the low-hung sun horizoned before him, his shadow a feverish paroxysm cast on the brindled land. The first bullet buckled his left leg and pitched him to the ground well before he heard the shot, its sonic sizzle a bullwhip cracked at his feet. Someone shouted. When he looked back, he saw the muzzle flashes coming from where they had ascended the highway embankment. The dirt sputtered and popped around him. He lifted himself and lurched into the thicket, his shot leg a leaden appendage, his left shoe gone. The second shot struck his shoulder with an impact that spun him onto his back. He lay as though pinned to the desert, the world a circle. When the third shot hit him, he heard nothing — not the sound of it, not the assailant's approach, not the click of the empty carbine near his head or the spatter of urine wetting him. Rugg did not feel the blade of the man's knife cut his toes.

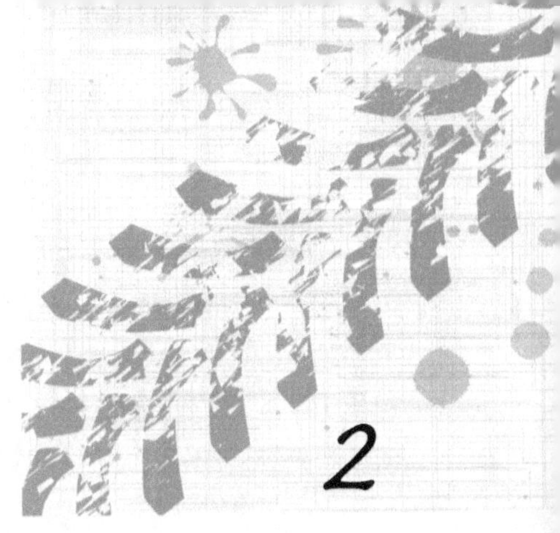

2

I ride in the bed of the gringo's truck, watching her pale face and crying eyes. Her vanilla hair. She sits between Chango and Tecolote inside the Cheyenne, which runs tight behind us. At the state line Chango pushes her to the floor, so the checkpoint inspectors won't notice as we drive through the gate. Then the Cheyenne passes us, and I don't see her.

We turn off at Talamantes and drive the dirt lateral until we cross the tracks. At the construction pits we unload the suitcases, a cooler, and fishing poles. We drink their canned Cokes from the cooler. Mencho opens the suitcases and dumps them on the ground. The gringa suitcase has a bikini and face paint and a package of tampons and red panties with white hearts. Inside a leather purse I find their dollars — fifties, twenties — traveling money, not a payout. The purse has their passports too, which I open *to look at the pictures. Her face has freckles and her teeth have braces and her hair is pulled in a ponytail. She looks like she hasn't lived a sad day in her life. Not one. Her old man, the gringo, looks like a minted cabrón. His picture has the same tough guy look I saw on his face. But that didn't save him. Anyway, tough is not how you look — the Mazatleco is tough and he has the sainted face of a baby hero.*

I throw the passports in the fire that Duende built to burn the truck papers pulled from the glove box. I throw in the gringo's wallet too. Mencho smashes their phones and computers, and he takes the plates off the truck, which is a white crew cab with four doors. White is our favorite boost. Four-door is good for unloading crews in a hurry. What we don't burn we throw into the pits. Besides the fishing poles there's a tackle box. Inside it are hooks, weights, bobbers, extra line — the whole show. I've always wanted to try fishing, but today isn't the start. We don't keep anything from our boosts. That's the rule. El Sin's rule. Nothing from the boosts. Nothing from the batos.

RUGG LAY WITH THE night unrolled above him, the land largely risen, a world evident. Then her name came to him.

Rose.

The ground cold where he lay. He remembered her bare feet, the nails painted pink.

No.

His feeble custody tossed aside without sacrifice. *Dad!* the last thing she had screamed.

Almighty God.

He glimpsed the jagged hem of the desert. He heard the highway's Doppler whine, the blacktop sneer of tires. The night otherwise silent.

Years before, Rugg had crashed a small plane into a jungle mountainside after the aircraft's empennage had failed under a gust load considerably more than the design limit. He had dragged himself two kilometers with multiple open fractures until he had found a clearing in the arboreal canopy where he had set a signal fire. Rugg knew broken. He knew the bone-splintered yaw, the hacked-out cry. He knew pain's fervent prayer.

He listened to the highway. He thought of his dead wife and where she lay buried, the ever-shadowed earth, the lawns, the pines. He thought of his dog. When he thought of Rose, he wept without murmur or tears. So Rugg lay, the stars whirling above him.

The day dawned when a bullrack operator climbed over the highway fence and carried his flattened roll of toilet paper into the scrub. He looked for snakes before he squatted. The snorts and squeals of the market swine he trucked broke the desert silence. The operator studied his boots and he surveilled his vicinity, the shadows sifted from the gray land. When he saw the shape that was Rugg, he took it for the sunken bulk of bagged trash, the contents spilled. Then he recognized a foot. He lifted his pants and sidled through the scrub to stare down at the body.

Enough light cast for him to see the blood splotches but not the wounds. He saw the man's shirt had been white. With his boot toe the operator nudged Rugg to no response. "Oye amigo, ¿estás bien?" The left shoe and sock gone. Toes missing. The smell of urine strong on him. He observed the luminous dial of a wristwatch. When he scanned the nearby scrub, he did not spot the shoe.

Twenty minutes down the highway, the bullrack operator parked beside the Telmex callbooth outside a roadside eatery. He dialed 066 to report that the body of a dead man lay approximately fifty meters off the south-bound lane of Highway 15, near kilometer post 83. The man shot or knifed, he said. When the emergency operator asked for his name and location, the driver hung up and returned to his truck.

The federal highway policemen who responded to the call spotted the brass casings on the shoulder. The big officer descended with binoculars to glass the expanse from the embankment where the shooters had stood, calculating how far a man could run through the scrub before the numbers overtook him. The sun up at the hour he spotted the shape of Rugg.

His weapon drawn as he advanced through the thicket beyond the fence. Clipped branches and a blooded shoe marked the fusillade. When he stood before Rugg, he holstered his weapon and removed a cell phone from his pocket. The dead man looked too big for a Mexican. Too pale. The big officer had seen enough shot Mexicans to know the dead ones kept their color, even after they bled out. He took pictures of Rugg's full length before he bent to frame a close-up of the face. In Rugg's nostrils blood sputum frothed with iridescent bubbles. The officer observed the man's chest, the shallow rise and fall of shirt buttons. He saw how the shoulder wound wept.

Back in the cruiser he drank water and checked phone messages before he radioed for an ambulance. After some minutes he retook the radio to request the coroner and the State Ministerial Police. He showed his junior officer the cell phone photos taken of Rugg. "They got his toes," he said.

The cops waited in the car, clocking the speed of passing motorists with a radar gun. When the Red Cross ambulance arrived, the big officer pointed the paramedics to where the gunshot man lay in the scrub. They were young medics, able-bodied and procedural, with volunteer patches sewn on their white uniforms. They dragged Rugg through the scrub to a workable clearing where they checked him for signs of life before moving him to the stretcher. They found his derangement in vitals consistent with stage 4 hypovolemic shock.

On the highway the big officer waited with a zipper storage bag on which he had written the date and the man's description: "Hombre — Tez Blanca." He ordered the medics to search the victim for identification. When they found nothing in the pockets, he told them to remove the man's watch and ring and to place them in the bag, which he handed to the ambulance driver with instructions that it accompany the victim to his destination, be it the hospital or the morgue. Then he released the ambulance. When the medical examiner and the ministerial agents arrived, the big officer reported that the victim had been resuscitated by the Red Cross medics and had departed in their ambulatory care. He indicated the spent casings on the roadside and the location where the unidentified male gunshot victim had fallen. He did not share the pictures taken with his cell phone.

In the ambulance the medics administered emergency oxygen and began aggressive fluid resuscitation with bagged intravenous saline solution stored in an ice cooler. The district Red Cross clinic had dispatched the ambulance without whole blood or plasma. The medics removed Rugg's remaining shoe before they cut off his shirt and pants. They applied compression bandages to the bullet wounds and secured a windless tourniquet on his gunshot leg. At the state line the ambulance was detained by a roadblock of farm tractors driven by local campesinos protesting the government-mandated price for field beans. When the protesters saw the flashing strobes, they opened an alley for the ambulance to pass.

Rugg arrived at the emergency entrance of the Hospital Civil suffering from severe hypotension and accidentally induced hypothermia caused by the infusion of cold fluids. The Red Cross medics removed their intravenous drip and resuscitation mask. They transferred Rugg to a hospital gurney where he was left uncovered in the access corridor with the storage bag tied to his wrist. The tourniquet they left on his leg. A charge nurse checked Rugg for a pulse and listened briefly to his heart. She untied the storage bag with the valuables and put it in her jacket pocket before she sided Rugg in a queue behind another ballistic trauma patient and two burn victims — brothers transported from a liquid ammonia accident.

He lay in a world swept of his presence. No one arrived to advocate for him or to advance his position in the queue. No family or friends stood vigilant. A phorid fly scuttled his length, circling the bandages and traversing his lips. It halted in the vestibule of Rugg's nostrils, its sensilla reading the whisper of Rugg's life in the shallow draft of his breath.

The smell of ammonia strong in the corridor. Rugg twenty-four hours bled when his vital signs were checked by the new charge nurse. She covered him with a disposable sheet too short to reach his feet and she called to an orderly dressed in street clothes, telling him to pull the gurney from the line. The family of the burned brothers watched Rugg's removal and the leisurely retreat of the gurney. The family numerous and with children, their voices hushed.

In the freight elevator the orderly lit a cigarette. He smoked without awareness of Rugg beyond the uncommon length of the man and his missing toes. The cigarette ashes he tipped outside the elevator's cage door. He waved away a fly. When the sheet abruptly creased at the man's lips as though bitten, the orderly dropped his cigarette. "¡Ay, carajo!" he blurted. At the service floor he got down and left Rugg on the elevator with the cage door lifted.

The second-year surgical resident who examined Rugg had been napping in the hospital warehouse when the orderly found him. He observed the crease mark in the sheet before he folded it back. After he pressed his ear to Rugg's chest, he asked the orderly for the cell phone holstered on his belt. The resident held the phone's lighted screen near Rugg's eyes, waiting for a pupillary response. He pointed to the elevator buttons. "Arriba," he told the orderly.

As the elevator ascended to the surgical floor, the resident appraised Rugg's wounds and the bristled stalks of thornbush stuck to his hair. He removed the windless tourniquet and wadded the disposable sheet into a cushion, using it to elevate the legs. The man's feet cold, the nail beds blanched on the remaining toes. The orderly gazed at Rugg. "Parece el Hombre Marlboro," he remarked, the conjecture prompted by the brand of cigarette he smoked. The resident watched the floors pass through the cage door, his first ride on the hospital's freight elevator. He said nothing. This idiot may have saved a life, he thought.

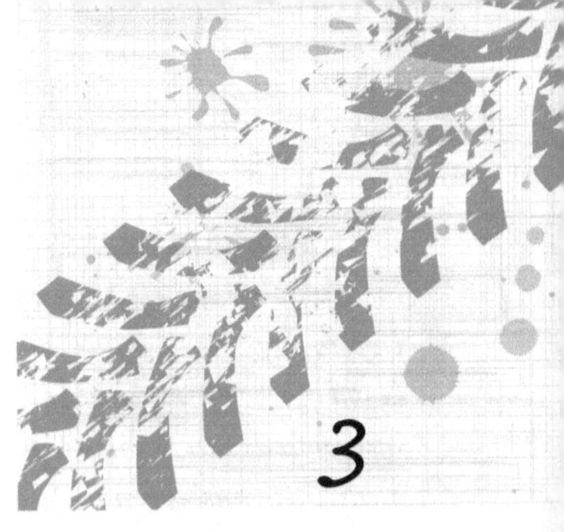

3

How I come to work for El Sin starts with me juggling for tips on the corner of Madero and Angel Flores. Before that I work as a window wipe, until my foot gets run over and heals crooked, which keeps me from outrunning other street wipes. I'm quick and tough, but after the accident, I'm just tough — tough with a limp. I learn to juggle from a Culichi kid whose old man got smoked by sicarios. He knows how to blow fire off a kerosene bottle and how to tumble on broken glass wearing nothing but his shorts. The glass he carries with him in a sack. It's a neat trick, not cutting himself, and it gets him good tips. He teaches me to juggle with tangerines, and then I upgrade to tennis balls after I steal a few from some kids in the park. The four-ball toss is my limit, which is enough to fetch interest at any intersection. Juggling for tips is just two-handed begging that passes for entertainment. A limp helps. When people see a kid doing something they can't do on two good feet, they get generous. Clean glass doesn't do that. As for the tips, they mostly keep me fed — and when they don't, I go to my aunt's house, where I get the usual welcome. Good-for-nothing slacker. Mother-shaming dog. Filthy, snot-nosed, burro, vagrant, plebe thief. She isn't a bad aunt, just bad-humored, which comes from having to concern herself with me, who showed up uninvited back when my stepdaddy ran me off for just cause after my mother died diabetic. Not even a sainted aunt is happy to see that kind of nephew. She's grouchy, but she never lets me starve. I'm fine with tortillas and salt. Or just tortillas. Sometimes that's all she has. She doesn't try to change me, which I like, and she lets me come and go without threats or sermons, only the name-calling. I hardly sleep there. Most nights I go to the park. When it's cold, an unlocked car works. I have a favorite bridge too, when it rains, but other street rats go there to sniff thinner from washrags. I'm not there yet — not a druggie, just a juggler.

Which gets me back to how I come to work for El Sin. I'm tossing balls at a red light at the corner of Madero and Angel Flores when a white Chevy Suburban stops and the tinted glass rolls down. "Hey kid," the driver says. "How much do you make doing that dumb trick?" It's a first for me — the first stupid question about juggling — but I don't say so. Instead, I say, "That's my business." The driver sits large behind the wheel. His face is dark and his head is too big for his Ray-Bans. There's a bato riding shotgun too. His face is scarred, and his wristwatch has jewels. There are others in the Suburban — I hear their voices — but the tinted glass hides them. The driver lowers his Ray-Bans to look at me. His eyes are bloodshot and sleepy. "Your business, eh?" he says. I tell him I own the balls, which makes it my business. He turns to the scarred bato. "Did you hear? He owns his balls." The scarred bato asks what's wrong with my foot. "My business," I answer. They laugh. I wait for them to drive off, but they don't. When the traffic light turns green, the Suburban sits, blocking the lane, while cars honk and traffic backs up behind it. The driver pulls a pistol from somewhere and flashes it out the window so the people in the cars can see it. It's a big pistol. Most of the honking stops. He looks at me and says something like — "Listen up, big man, the cops are cleaning the streets. We pay five hundred a day. There's room for one more." He rolls down the rear window, and I see who's inside. Two batos ride in the back. They've got pistols too. Between them sits a kid. Three more kids sit in the third row. One is a wipe I recognize, and he recognizes me. "Rayo, get in," he says. That's my nickname. Rayo. It means speedy — like a thunderbolt — because I can't run with my bad foot. The driver breaks out a cigarette. The light turns red. "Five hundred to do what?" I ask. He grins. "Errands," he answers, "you know — errands." What I know is that five hundred pesos buys a lot of errands. I say, "You mean, errands like running for tortillas?" He laughs. "Yeah, tortillas," he says. Then he tells me that juggling balls isn't the same as wearing a pair. I tell him I'm working on that. When I tell him only mafiosos pay five hundred pesos to run errands, he stops grinning and spits out the window, almost hitting me. Then he says something that does hit me. He says, "That kind of money makes up for who you aren't, kid, and right now you're nothing — nothing but a trick with a limp — so get in or get lost before the cops shut that big mouth of yours." I already know about the cops. It's street news. The wipe who knows me holds up a tall bottle of Coca-Cola that he and the other kids share in the back seat. "Rayo, it's cold," he says. I look at him. From nothing he has gone to all he wants. The sun beats down. I'm thirsty. The Coke looks half full. "Move over," I say. Then I drop the tennis balls and limp in. That's how it starts.

RUGG GAZED AT THE whitewashed windows.

"¿Me oye?" asked the girl who stood looking down at him, her black hair tucked under a nurse's cap.

He nodded. Wire arches cinched his jaw. Blood seeped from his mouth. His left foot amputated.

She inserted a straw in the tooth gap. "Tómalo," she said. Rugg drank, the water warm. When he finished, the nurse timed his pulse using her wristwatch before she listened to his chest with a single-sided stethoscope. Rugg lay naked under the sheet. He looked at her watch, seeing no second hand. The pain large below his knee. His other wounds dwarfed by the devouring blaze. The nurse checked the catheter in his hand and she tapped the drip chamber on the IV line. "¿Todo bien?" she asked. He nodded. Not a question he could answer any other way.

The bed wet where he sweated. Dried blood on the sheets. Rugg fixed his gaze on the plaster cracks overhead, the pictures it drew. He saw the face of Rose and he saw the face of mayhem. Nothing else drawn.

The doctor who came wore blue scrubs. His mustache a thin ellipse that accented a refined and presumptive air.

He lifted the taped gauze from Rugg's neck to examine the bullet's deep graze. "Qué suerte con esta bala," he remarked. He reapplied the dressing before he removed the bandage from Rugg's shoulder and checked the wound. He nodded approvingly. From Rugg's amputated leg he unwound the compression bandage, then sniffed the stump. "Muy bien," he observed. Rugg let the doctor rewrap the leg before he motioned for the chart clipboard hung on the bedpost. The board with a nub pencil tied to a string. What information to share with this doctor a thing Rugg had already considered. On the chart's front page he wrote his name and pointed to himself. The doctor read it. "Bob Rugg? Very good. We were waiting until you could speak."

Rugg knew the perils of survival. Should Rose's abductors learn that he was hospitalized, gone the advantage to surprise them and recover her. Their opportunity to kill him gifted again. He did not know what the cops would do.

"Gringo solo," he wrote, showing it to the doctor.

He smiled. "You are not alone, Mr. Rugg. You are in our capable hands."

Rugg waited. The doctor said nothing about another gringo in the hospital. Nothing about Rose. The likelihood large, Rugg thought, that his daughter's abduction unknown to this doctor and to those who had brought him here. He wrote. "¿Accidente?"

The doctor showed surprise. He made a pistol with his hand and pointed it at Rugg's leg. "No accident. You do not remember?" Rugg lied with his head. The doctor said he did not know the circumstances of Rugg's ordeal, only that he had been shot and brought to the hospital in critical condition. He called Rugg a lucky man. "You have much luck to be alive, Mr. Rugg. I am sorry I could not save your foot. The fractures and severed toes made it beyond repair. Your jaw break, however, has no fragmentation, which is excellent news."

Rugg took in the doctor's face. This man's measure of fortuity gauged by what mortal lesions a patient could outlive. He gripped the pencil. "¿Dónde estoy?" he wrote.

"You are in the Hospital Civil of Los Mochis," the doctor answered. Then he introduced himself. "I am Dr. Sanchez."

A blurred map sketched in Rugg's head of where he lay and where they had stopped him on the highway. He wrote on the chart. "No tengo dinero."

Dr. Sanchez told Rugg the hospital was a public benefit institution and, as such, he would not pay until he had the money.

Rugg was unsure what that meant. He pointed to the doctor's pants. He lifted the sheet to show his nakedness. He wrote "¿Ropa?"

The doctor told him that he would get clothes soon. Rugg held to the clipboard. He regarded the cell phone on the doctor's hip, a Motorola with a whip antenna and a strip display.

From across the ward a young man cried out. His burned and blistered skin raw and undressed. "¡Hermano,

hermano!" he wailed. Two children sat on his bed. Near him a woman wept. The doctor regarded them. When he inquired if Rugg had family in Mexico, Rugg shook his head.

"Family is important," the doctor observed, and then he told Rugg that should he need anything, the staff was at his orders. Rugg made a walking gesture with his fingers. Dr. Sanchez smiled. His thin mustache drew a line. "You will walk again, Mr. Rugg. We have good prosthetics here, handmade and custom-fitted. But first, let's get you to speak. The wires must come out."

Rugg wrote nothing. When the doctor left, he flipped back through the chart to the first page, counting eight days. They would have been at the beach today, Rose sunburned and happy. He with fish.

He set the clipboard on the bed. The drugged gavillero recalled, his knife. Severed toes, the doctor had said. *Sonofabitch.*

The harrowed wails of distant patients reached Rugg. From the adjacent bed a soul-rattling sough rose from a gray-haired man who lay beneath a sheet. A young woman sat at his side. She clutched prayer beads and spoke softly with breathless intensity. Rugg heard "Dios" and "Cristo." Later the smell of excrement reached him from where the burned youth defecated stiffly into a bedpan, his family attempting to screen him. The ward without curtains or ceiling fans.

The pain in Rugg's leg the way he imagined a dull hatchet hacked bone. A hell beyond manhandled, the hours without measure. He lay before a white-windowed day, his eyes closed to its light. That night he saw her shoeless feet. He saw the soiled hands of men, the silver hair of the boss, his handsome face. In the darkness a woman spoke above him, the name Jesús whispered. He heard the click of beads. So he lay, hung in an endless night, the fallen world pressed upon him. His life a torn dream.

Rugg a stranger to himself days later when they brought him a mirror to shave. His bearded face a mask of broken and bruised flesh, his jaw not quite aligned. After Rugg razored, a youth came to his bedside. He identified himself as a dental intern. With a surgical side cutter he removed the wire arches, pulling each from between the teeth. No murmur rose from Rugg, his gaze fixed on the plaster cracks overhead. After the wires were pulled, the intern gave him a cup of water and a spitting bowl to rinse his mouth. Rugg drank and swallowed, the blood tasting of metal, the wired tightness clinging to his teeth. He felt an uneven crossbite, but he said nothing to the intern, answering with a nod when asked if he desired food.

They brought him a bowl with corn tortillas torn into bite-size pieces and softened in bean broth. Rugg ate with his fingers, no spoon brought with the bowl. The young woman who sat with the gray-haired man ate tacos off a disposable plate. The tacos topped with shredded lettuce. She placed two in Rugg's bowl. "No es comida," she said, speaking of what Rugg ate.

Rugg thanked her, the words stiffly mouthed. He nodded toward the gray-haired man. "¿Padre?"

"Sí," she said. "Tiene cáncer."

Rugg ate. No counsel came to him. To each his own misery was a truth he would not share with this woman. The tacos stuffed with meat and fried potatoes. He pointed to the whitewashed windows and asked if they were on the first floor.

The woman shook her head. She held up three fingers.

Rugg nodded. "¿Hay taxi?"

"En la esquina," she answered.

"¿De noche?"

"Sí, de noche."

When the doctor made his rounds, Rugg opened his mouth. "I speak. I leave," he said. Dr. Sanchez smiled. He apologized for his ignorance of English, except in the written form. Rugg said, "Ya me voy."

"No, no," the doctor replied. He said a nurse would remove the shoulder and neck stitches in a few days. He examined the leg, bending it at the knee to give Rugg a look at the limb. Rugg saw the swollen, transposed flaps of skin, the seeping sutures. "Dos semanas," the doctor said. He made the same walking gesture Rugg had made with his fingers.

Two weeks hell, Rugg told himself. "Where are my clothes and shoes?" he asked.

The doctor said the clothes had likely been destroyed for sanitary reasons. He promised a hospital gown in short order.

Rugg pointed to the compression mark left on his finger by the wedding band. "What about my ring?" He tapped his wrist. "My watch?" He had mimed the same inquiry to the nurses, each shrugging ignorance. Rugg was certain the gavillero who had lifted his wallet had left untouched the ring and watch. The boyish figure framed in memory. His crooked mask, the flashy sneakers, his limp. Images saved for when Rugg found him.

Dr. Sanchez called the disappearance of personal property unacceptable. The hospital administrator would be notified, he said. He suggested Rugg make a list.

"If you think leaving me naked will keep me here, you don't know me," Rugg said. "As soon as my daughter is safe, I'll be back to pay the bill and to shoot you for taking off my foot."

The doctor apologized again for his ignorance of English.

Rugg nodded. He thanked the doctor for his frank admission of incompetency.

That afternoon the nurse brought the hospital gown. When she asked Rugg if he needed help attiring, he waved her away. He dressed and swung his good leg off the bed. The amputated limb he inched over the edge, weathering the blood-descended jackhammer. He clutched the mattress with both hands as he sat, the cries of all men before him commiserating between clenched teeth. Minutes passed before he gripped the IV pole and lowered himself to the floor. The daughter of the ill man watched from her chair. "Cuidado," she said. Rugg balanced on his good foot, waiting for the dizziness to pass. The IV pole rode on swivel casters that rolled with Rugg as he hopped. His stumped limb he bent at the knee, though it easily cleared the floor. He circled the bed and sat, sweating and out of breath, unable to remember the last time he had hopped on one leg.

He waited before he stood again. When he hopped out of the ward, a nurse appeared and told him to return to his bed.

"Go to hell," Rugg said. He surveilled the corridor before he turned around. The nurse's station adjacent to the ward. At the end of the corridor a SALIDA sign affixed above double doors. The sign with a red arrow that pointed down.

Later he hopped to the ward restroom. The IV pole too tall to wheel past the door, but the feeder line long enough for Rugg to enter and straddle the toilet. The door without a lock. No toilet paper in the holder. On the wall a glass-doored cabinet with a key lock. The shelves stocked with bottles of iodine, gauze pads, and rolled tape. Rugg lifted the hospital gown and squatted. He stared at his bandaged stump, the hemic wad. When he returned to his bed, the burned brother cried out to him, "¡Hermano, hermano!" His blackened head and blistered body reminded Rugg of a burned man he had flown from a forest blaze, the man a bulldozer operator sucked from his machine by a firestorm tornado, his cries not to a brother but to God.

Rugg lay with his leg sheet-wrapped, a combustive devouring where no foot protruded. The ward still daylit when a patient on crutches stopped before Rugg's bed to grin at him. "Gringo mocho," he gibed. The patient younger than Rugg, his legs with feet. When he retreated, Rugg eyed the crutches.

That night the moaning from the next bed ceased. Rugg slept, the first dreams come to him — the face of his dead wife, the tanned legs of Rose chasing the dog. In the morning the gray-haired man gone, the mattress stripped. The chair where the woman had sat pushed next to Rugg's bed. On it lay folded clothes, packaged underwear, a single shoe. Inside the shoe a wadded paper. When Rugg opened it, he found a tightly creased fifty-peso bill. The paper with a handwritten note. "Que Dios te cuide," it read.

Rugg sized the shirt and jeans. The clothes laundered and pressed. The shoe a well-worn huarache with a tire sole and buckle straps. He removed the undershorts from the plastic bag and set them with the sandal on the chair. The bag he put beneath his pillow. The fifty-peso bill he rolled and slipped between the tape and the butterfly catheter affixed to his arm. He read the note again, the kindness of this beset stranger framed in faith. When the nurse arrived to remove the stitches, he asked, "¿El viejo?" He pointed to where the old man had lain. The nurse shrugged. "Se fue," she said. Gone — to home, to grave, to God, to the devil — not her elaboration to make. Rugg motioned for the scissors that lay on the surgical tray. "Por favor," he said. She handed him the scissors, and Rugg cut six inches off the left pantleg of the jeans and slit the inseam to the knee. He kept the cutoff piece. After the nurse left, he lay watching the man on crutches walk the ward. Rugg watched him until the man returned to his bed.

When the doctor saw the clothes and the sandal, he congratulated Rugg on his readiness. "Mi familia," Rugg lied. The doctor examined the amputated limb. "Excelente progreso," he pronounced. Rugg said he needed a stronger pain medication. He exaggerated the discomfort in his leg. Dr. Sanchez nodded, agreeing to prescribe a more potent analgesic.

The nurse brought the blue capsules in a paper pill cup. "Toma," she said. Rugg put the capsules in his mouth and drank the water she had given him. The nurse waited until he swallowed. When she departed, he spat the capsules into the pill cup. Sleeping through hell not a road out of here, he decided. He wadded the cup with the capsules and put it in the pocket of the gifted shirt.

At the hour the ward filled with visitors, Rugg retook the IV pole and hopped to the restroom with the under-wear and the pants under his arm. He carried the jeans cutoff in the plastic bag. Inside the room he clamped the IV fluid drip and balanced against the wall. With the cutoff over his hand, he broke the cabinet glass with a punctuated jab. He listened. No silence fell over the clamor of the visitors outside. Rugg extracted the largest piece of glass from the frame and took from the cabinet a handful of gauze pads, rolls of adhesive, and a bottle of iodine, placing the items in the plastic bag. The piece of glass he slid back inside the cabinet. He sat on the toilet and removed one of the gauzes from its paper wrap. With his teeth he tore off a short length of tape and stuck it to his knee before he lifted the adhesive that held the catheter to his arm. Rugg took the rolled fifty-peso bill the woman had given him and cornered it in his mouth. The catheter he pulled from the vein, affixing the gauze pad over the needle puncture with the tape. To pull on the undershorts he cleared his buttocks by arching against the toilet tank. He struggled with the pants. So many mornings the job done without thought or toil. When he stood, the jeans loose in the waist. He pulled the tie from the gown and threaded it through the belt loops before knotting it. The plastic bag he tucked under the waist tie. A knock on the restroom door caught Rugg with the fifty-peso bill in his mouth. "Momento," he grunted. He reaffixed the catheter to the outside of his taped arm. When he opened the door, the crutched walker stood there. "¡Qué chingados, gringo!" he blurted. Rugg said nothing. He retook the IV pole and hopped to his bed, the plastic bag under the gown. The ward still crowded with visitors. In bed, he lay under the sheet with the drip clamp closed on the intravenous line, the fifty-peso bill pushed into the pants pocket.

The ward dark when he sat up, the whitewashed windows ghosted with gray light. He removed the sham catheter and tied the tubing to the IV pole before he slipped out of the gown. The gifted shirt he sleeved first over his wounded shoulder, the tails left untucked when he buttoned the front. He lowered himself to the chair where the woman had sat. He lifted his good leg and buckled on the sandal, the leather well-fitted, as though Rugg had tread upon it in another life. He sat in the chair with his gaze turned to the corner bed, its sheeted shape.

The sandal's tire sole silent on the tiled floor. Rugg crossed the ward without the IV pole, one-footedness preferred to the noise of casters jumping the grouted joints. He hopped and stopped, then hopped again, holding to bedframes, his shadow momentarily cast upon the fitful and slumbered. At the corner bed he gazed down at the man who had called him gringo. The man's arm flung across his face, a stertorous discord fouling his sleep. Rugg took the crutches that lay beside the bed. He retreated from the corner before he slipped them under his arms. Wooden crutches, the handgrips loose, the uprights shortened for a smaller man. Rugg not new to crutches but new to the phantom feel of one-sided footfalls. He made his way to the chair, where he retrieved the plastic bag with the medical supplies, snugging it under the waist tie. The ward behind him as the burned brother cried out for his flesh and blood. "¡Hermano, hermano!"

Rugg paused at the entrance.

"¡Hermano!" the brother cried again before a woman's wearied whisper hushed him.

From the nurse's station faint music drifted into the corridor. The SALIDA sign lit, the rooms dark as Rugg advanced. At the end of the corridor he found the stairs. He gripped the handrail as he descended, holding the crutches with his free hand. Three floors, the woman had said. The stairwell windowless, the shaft dimly lit, Rugg's shadow a stick-figured shape pitched across the grimed walls. He saw Rose running on a white beach, her barefooted prints left in the wet sand. *Sonofabitches.* At the second-floor landing he halted to pull up the jeans, his leg throbbing, the dressing darkly splotched. He retied the waist cord before he resumed his descent, the single-sandaled footfalls reverberating heavily on the concrete steps. Cool air wafted into the stairwell from the first-floor landing. The corridor empty when he entered, the exit door glassed. Beyond it, the streetlighted night.

The taxis queued on a corner, as the woman had told him. He crutched to the first car and rapped on the passenger window, waking the driver, who came around to open the rear door. When Rugg chinned his preference to ride shotgun, the driver slid the bucket seat rearward. "For the crutches," he explained. Rugg nodded, no irony too small to ignore at this hour. Inside the taxi the seasoned scent of pine forests. Rugg asked the driver to take him to a cheap hotel, one with phones in the rooms. He pulled the fifty-peso bill from his pocket. "Todo mi dinero," he said, showing it. The driver did not ask how Rugg would pay for a room. He said he would charge thirty pesos, the hotel nearby.

Rugg cranked down the door glass. Nogales the last place he had felt window wind on his face. They had crossed the border when Rose pinched her nose. "Eww, gross!" she had exclaimed. "Sewage," he had told her. "Get used to it, girl."

Outside the taxi window, the same smell.

He read the time on the dash clock. When he asked the driver the day, the driver said, "Sunday." He did not look at Rugg. He said nothing about Rugg's leg or his accent. A gringo with one foot and fifty pesos bound for a cheap hotel before daybreak prompted no query. Such were his fares, such the travails of men. He drove, humming to himself.

"Hay Western Union aquí?" Rugg asked.

"Telégrafos," the driver replied.

"¿Abierto?"

The driver said the telegraph office, being a good-for-nothing government agency, was not open on Sundays.

Rugg stared out the window. Sue will pick up today, he thought. After church.

When the taxi arrived at the hotel, the driver apologized for being unable to make change for the fifty-peso bill. Rugg told him to keep it. Then he descended and retook the crutches.

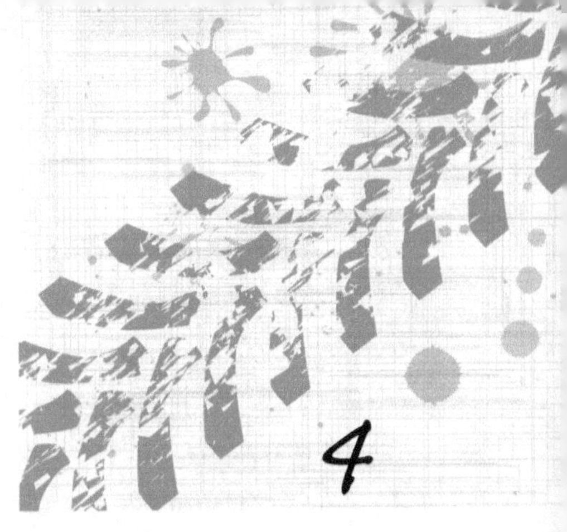

4

The bato wearing the Ray-Bans is Macho Prieto. The one with the scarred face and fancy watch is Zuky. They're right about the cops. A week after I get in the Suburban, the police clean the streets of wipes, jugglers, shines, and any kid who can't outrun them, which would have been me. Most go to the county houses, where they get to eat but work for it. The youngest go to Santa Eduwiges, a kids' home run by tough nuns and a queer priest. Every street kid knows about the priest. Me and the other kids in the Suburban go to live in a gated crash house where we run errands for five hundred pesos a day. I'm right about the tortillas. We run for breakfast tacos too, and menudo, ice, Cokes, snacks, and cigarettes. A lot of cigarettes. Macho Prieto runs the house and the crew. Zuky is his second. Twenty batos camp in the house, coming and going at all hours, smelling of beer and gunfire. On the floor are mattresses where they sleep. Me and the other kids bring food and clean up what's left after twenty batos treat a house like a bus terminal. No one cooks, or mops floors, or cleans toilets — this isn't a normal house — but we throw the trash in the backyard and we squash any roaches we see, which are plentiful. We eat what the crew eats, if there are leftovers, and we watch a TV with a built-in cassette player. The cassettes have churro movies with gunfighters and sheriffs and Indians shooting it out in the Old West, which are my favorites.

Some of the batos want to know why I limp. When I say I was run over by a car while chasing a tip, they laugh. Zuky asks, "Hey, dumbass, did you get the make and model?" I say, "No, but I got the tire. A Goodyear radial." Even Macho Prieto laughs, and MP doesn't laugh at much. Zuky calls me a dumbass again. He likes the name, and I don't have an opinion. My job is following whatever orders come down from MP. Call it starting at the bottom. I don't need to know MP's business to know it's dirty. Knowing too much too soon is never a good thing when you hold to the bottom rung on the ladder of crime. All I need to know is what I see, and what I see are guns, cash, and cars coming and going. I also know that five hundred pesos a day isn't forever, which is why I spend my cash like there's no tomorrow. I buy shirts and pants and baseball caps and pairs of colored sneakers, a pocket knife, a gold neck chain, *and a watch with four buttons. I satisfy all my street food hungerings for tortas, birria, ceviche, churros, and stick ice cream. At times I eat until I get sick, which says a lot about me and consequences. Some mistakes I repeat to get the most out of a bad choice.*

One morning Zuky says, "MP wants you on a corner. Get in the car." I say, "What corner?" He says, "Don't ask, dumbass. Get in the car." I get in, and he takes me to the corner of Carranza and Belisario. I know the place from my windshield wiping days. Zuky points to a car wash on the corner and says, "Get down and count the cars they wash." I say, "OK. You want the wax jobs too?" He gives me a chiller look that shuts me up. "Same thing tomorrow," he says. "Take a bus." I get down and count the washed cars that drive away. I buy oranges from a bicycle vendor and move to the corner where I juggle to avoid looking unemployed. One hundred and eighty-four cars get washed in two days. I give Zuky the tally, and a week later he drops me off in front of a seafood restaurant where I count the customers coming to eat. There's a line out the door. I figure the food must be free or at least good. When I give Zuky the numbers, he grins and says, "I didn't know you could count that high." I bite down on a smartass reply because the job gets me out of the house and I make five hundred pesos a day to do nothing but count. I go to a Pemex station to tally the cars gassing up. I stand in front of a hardware store counting the walk-ins. Then Zuky sends me to the alley behind an appliance store and tells me to count the delivery trucks leaving the dock. That afternoon, a bato from the store comes over to ask my business. "Nothing," I say. He's a young type dressed like management. He says, "You tell him the deal is done." I ask, "Tell who?" He says, "Who sent you, that's who. I know what you are doing." I give him my dumbass look. "Then you know more than I do," I say. He says, "You tell him my dad says the deal is done. You tell him that." His bark is loud, but his eyes are scared. I've seen it in dogs. Then he says, "Get out of here before I call the cops." When I start to limp away, he says, "If you come back, I'll break the other leg." I deliver the message to Zuky, but he doesn't want the details. Instead, he asks how many delivery trucks I counted. I tell him, and he asks, "How about the trucks you didn't count because you left?" I don't have an answer, so I shrug. When he gives me his chiller look, I know I screwed up. Right away he sends me back to house chores. I figure it's the end of me climbing the ladder. I hardly see MP. Zuky gives the orders. A few days later, a radio is turned on in one of the rooms, and an announcer gives the news. He talks about a woman who buys a new refrigerator that gets delivered to her house. The delivery men put it in her kitchen, and when the woman opens the door, she finds a man's head inside. The woman recognizes him. The head belongs to the man who sold her the refrigerator. Turns out, he is the son of the owner of the appliance store. The radio announcer doesn't give the name of the store, but I know I've been there — to the back of it — and I think the management bato who threatened to break my leg won't be breaking it. I knew he looked scared — the dog look doesn't lie.

Weeks pass before Zuky speaks to me again. I'm dumping disposables in a vacant lot across the street when he comes up and points to my watch. "Do you know how to tell time, dumbass?" he asks. I'm the only kid wearing a watch. I give him the hour. He checks his fancy watch. It's got jewels, but the time is the same. "Get in the car," he says, and just like that I'm back on the street. My first job is to clock a bato who visits the same hotel every day. The bato is fat, and the hotel looks old. I check the hours he comes and leaves. The guy is a regular. Maybe he lives there. Maybe he owns it. I buy a pocket notebook, where I write down the times. Later I tear out the sheets and give them to Zuky. It's a simple business. I clock batos leaving their houses. I clock batos going to bars. I clock a woman who picks up her kid at school. I clock cabs. I clock cops. I go through a lot of notebooks. Then Zuky gives me a phone — not a fancy one but it has a clip holster. The phone is for calling Zuky — only Zuky. His number is on the screen.

When I press the Call button, he doesn't answer, but he knows that whoever I'm clocking has left or arrived or is on the move. I don't make any other calls, and no one calls me. I do a lot of cop watching. If I see a municipal patrol, I ring his number once. If the cops are ministerial, twice. For the feds, three rings. Soldiers, four. Every week Zuky switches out my phone for another just like it. He carries a satchel with phones. Also, he has a stash of license plates, which I steal for him. He tells me that such-and-such car is parked at such-and-such place — a Lobo with frontier plates, a Navigator from Jalisco. Mostly I steal out-of-state plates, but also plates from the cars that gringos park on side streets. I carry a stub screwdriver and a pocket wrench. Zuky says I'm the fastest plate thief he's seen — for a cripple — which I don't take as a compliment.

One night I'm on a mattress at the house when MP comes in. He wears his Ray-Bans indoors. He sees me and says, "How much are you carrying?" I pull a wad from my pocket, all five hundreds. "You see," he says. "You got more than a limp." He sends me to buy cigarettes, and when I return, I make conversation. "Smoking causes cancer," I say — as a joke, not a warning — because any idiot can read the package. MP breaks out a butt, lights it, and takes a pull. He blows the smoke from the side of his mouth. "It won't be cigarettes that kill me," he says. And he's right.

A few days later, MP is killed, no cigarettes involved. For us at the bottom of the ladder, the news is old when we hear it. Word comes down that MP is lifted by El Sin's crew on the Leyva Boulevard, his body dumped in a cane break, where the cops find him wrapped in a falsa blanket — some of him busted, some of him missing, all of him a message — what happens to batos who don't turn over business to El Sin. I feel lousy for MP, having to go that way, but not lousy enough to show it or to go to his burial. That's for friends and family, which I'm not. Two flavors of bad guys go to a bad guy's funeral — those who go to comfort the relatives and those who go to ambush them. I don't belong to either. When we get the official word on new management, it's from Zuky, who leaves out the details. "MP is done," he says. "We work for El Sin now." No one asks the why or the what-for.

I've heard of El Sin. I've heard he runs a big crew. The first time I see him we are out of the city and moved into a house in El Carrizo, a highway town near the state line. One morning he shows up, and not alone. He has an escort — large rides, late models. When the tinted windows roll down, I see the batos inside. They wear masks and flash hardware. One of our crew says, "That's him." Only one bato sits without a mask, and he doesn't get down. Zuky leaves his breakfast and goes to him. They talk at the window. El Sin has a boy face. His hair is silver and cut to the floor. I watch him without watching him. What happened to MP keeps my eyes cornered. When Zuky returns, he points to me and says, "You and Cachoro ride with them." Cachoro is older than me and more traveled, like a suitcase. He's a driver and the cousin of some big-shot federal cop. He asks Zuky, "What's down, man?" Zuky answers, "Orders, ox." Nothing spills from my mouth. Wear 'em is what I do. I limp to the street. El Sin has his window down. I know he's watching me, but I don't look at him. I hear the doors unlock and I hear him say, "Get in, kid." That's how I come to ride with him.

A one-word neon sign hung above the entrance: HOTEL. The small lobby furnished with a single chair occupied by an old man who slept under a baseball cap. On his feet walk-worn huaraches.

The clerk waited for Rugg to approach the desk. "We don't have an elevator," he said.

Rugg paired the crutches and stood them by the desk. On the counter sat a push-button phone with a hardwired handset. Rugg asked if the rooms had phones.

"No," replied the clerk. He told Rugg that guests used the lobby phone, that local calls were free. He placed a pen and registration card before Rugg.

Nearby, a letter board displayed the rates. A room with air-conditioning more expensive than one without it. At the bottom of the board the payment terms written in uppercase: ¡No Hay Credito!

The clerk said there was guest parking behind the building, but the hotel did not assume liability for vehicle theft or damage. Rugg said he had come by taxi. He took the pen and filled out the card, writing his name and address, his sister's home phone number. He left blank the number of days he intended to lodge. Then he set down the pen. On the wall hung a picture calendar of a sunlit beach. Rugg regarded the weeks lost. *A goddamn eternity.*

Behind the desk sat an analog telefax on a folding card table. Next to it stood a mailroom cabinet with cubicles that held the room keys, the hotel mostly vacant. When the clerk asked if he wanted a room with air-conditioning, Rugg replied, "I have a problem." He explained that he carried no money.

The clerk's face without surprise, as though claims of destitution were a familiar narrative at this hour. "Yes," he agreed. "That is a problem."

Rugg made a gun with his hand. "Robbed," he said. "My wallet. My watch." He raised his arm to show his bare wrist.

"Ah," said the clerk. "For that you want a free room?"

"No," Rugg answered. "Credit for one day."

The clerk pointed to the old man asleep in the chair. "Our free room," he said. "You must fight him for it."

Rugg nodded. What he would have said had he been a night clerk with a man asleep in the only lobby chair. "Monday I'll have the money telegraphed," he told the clerk.

The clerk said the hotel was going nowhere, that it would be here when the gentleman returned Monday with the money.

Rugg offered to sign a promissory note.

The clerk shook his head. He said the biggest lie in Mexico was tomorrow I pay you.

"OK," Rugg said. His leg ached. He did not look at the bandage. He read the time on the wall clock. "May I make a collect call?" he asked.

The clerk replied that only guests could make calls, collect or otherwise. When Rugg said the call was to request money to pay the hotel, the clerk shrugged. He retrieved Rugg's registration card and stuck it in one of the cubicles.

Rugg retook the crutches and turned to the door. He had no plan. The old man sat awake in the chair. "You're leaking, friend," he said. He pointed to the blood splotches on the floor where Rugg stood.

The clerk peered over the desk. He left the lobby and returned with a mop. He told Rugg to go to the hospital.

The old man rose from the chair. "Sit," he offered. "You are pruned. I am whole. Sit."

After Rugg sat, he set the crutches on the floor and pulled from under his shirt the bag with the medical supplies. The old man watched as Rugg lifted the stump onto his knee to tape more gauze pads over the wound.

"It looks fresh cut," the old man said.

Rugg nodded.

"At least you came prepared."

When Rugg finished, he placed the bag beneath his shirt. He looked at the man's baseball cap. "The Dodgers have a good team," he said.

The old man laughed. "Good for nothing."

Rugg knew baseball. He pointed to his eyes to show what he had seen with them. "Fernando Valenzuela, 1981

World Series." He did not mention that on the drive south he had passed the highway turnoff to the famed pitcher's hometown of Etchohuaquila. An hour before hell had found them.

The old man looked impressed. He asked Rugg how he came to be at the hotel with a cut-off leg.

"Don't be nosy, Father," interjected the desk clerk.

Rugg made the gun with his hand, the same gesture he had made for the son. The old man's eyes widened. "¿Sicarios?"

"Please, Father."

Their faces made Rugg cautious. "Bandidos," he corrected, opting for outlawry stripped of barbarity.

"Ah!" said the old man. "They robbed you?"

"Yes," Rugg answered. "Money. Truck. Everything." He did not mention Rose.

"Your truck too?"

"Yes."

He pointed to Rugg's leg. "So, they shot you?"

Rugg nodded.

"And the police know?"

"I do not know what the police know," Rugg replied.

The old man told Rugg that the police would do nothing. "They are dead men swimming. They pass with their eyes open, but they see nothing."

Rugg silent.

"My name is Pedro Martínez," the old man said. "That is my son, Pedrito. He is the night manager."

Rugg gave his name.

Pedro Martínez held out his hand for Rugg to shake. "I am sorry for your misfortune, Mr. Rugg. You came to visit Mexico?"

"Yes."

"Terrible! What dirty luck!" The old man turned to his son. "Pedrito, you should give this man a room. He is a stranded foreigner with one foot."

Young Pedro told his father that if the rooms were free, the foreigner would be sleeping in one and so would he.

The old man tapped his elbow. "My son is a hard one," he whispered. "Like his mother."

Rugg rested the amputated leg on his knee, watching the gauze pads spot.

"Let this foreigner make his phone call. I will pay," the old man told his son.

"He is not a guest, Father."

"Make him a guest. I will pay."

"You have no money."

"My brother will allow it."

"Call him," Pedrito said.

The old man bent near Rugg before he spoke. "My brother owns this hotel. He is Pedrito's boss, but he never comes." On the old man's face Rugg saw blue sky and amusement. Life's worries long absent from his lively eyes.

"My call is collect," he said. "To get money. No one pays."

The old man went to the phone. "Pedrito," he said, "let him call for money. You have empty rooms. That is bad for business, bad for you. Do you want to go back to washing dishes?"

Rugg listened. How his father had implored him to clean the horse stalls. "Clean them, son, or shoe shitted horses."

Young Pedro threw up his hands. "Rápido," he said before he retreated behind the mailroom cabinet.

Rugg retook the crutches and stood. He asked Pedro if he carried photo identification.

"Absolutely," he answered. "I am plainly identified."

When Rugg asked to see it, the old man handed over a voter registration card. In the photo Pedro grinned.

"That's me," he said. "I just voted. Picked the loser."

Rugg said he had no wallet, no passport. He told the old man he would pay him to use his identification. "To receive the telegraphed money."

"No need to pay me," Pedro said. "Favors are done for free, aren't they, Pedrito?"

Young Pedro remained silent. Rugg took the phone and pressed zero. When the operator asked who was authorized to accept the charges, Rugg gave his sister's name.

The phone rang. He looked at the clock. His own worst fear realized in a call like this on another predawn morning. When she answered, he said, "Sue. It's Bob. I have a problem."

She took a moment to surface. "Bob, it's three ..."

"I know. I had an accident."

He waited.

"Accident? Your truck?"

"Yeah. I need you to wire money."

"Is Rose all right?"

His answer prepared: "She'll be fine. Can you get to the Western Union in Lawton? It's on your way to church."

"Of course." Her voice fully awakened. "I don't need to go to church."

"On West Gore. In the Country Mart. It should be open but check the hours. I need the money first thing Monday."

"You lost your money in the accident?"

"Yeah. It's a long story. I'm going to give you the name of the wire recipient and the address. It's Spanish. You need to write it down."

"I took Spanish, Bob. Let me get the light."

He read the old man's name off the voting card. Then he gave her the city and state. She read it back to him. When she asked for the amount, Rugg said the maximum payout for an international wire was ten thousand dollars. "Send that."

"Ten thousand? Why so much? Who is this man, Bob?"

Rugg could see her free hand riding the edge of her voice. Always the older sister.

"I can't cash a wire sent in my name. He's helping me."

"Can you trust him?"

"Sue, please. Wire the money. They'll take a card."

Hesitation. "OK. But I don't understand why you can't cash it."

"I don't have an ID. I lost my passport and license."

"In the accident?"

"Yes."

"Jesus, Bob."

He told her where to find the signed checks in the house. He gave her the hotel number, reading it off the telephone base plate.

"What hotel? What's your room number?"

Rugg said he didn't have a room yet. He gave her the country code for Mexico and told her to call him with the wire confirmation number.

"Isn't it dangerous to carry that kind of cash down there? I heard …"

"Sue."

"OK."

He asked her to get the phone number of the American Consulate in Hermosillo, Sonora.

"Where is that?"

"It's the nearest consulate. Don't call them. Check online. It's a duty phone for US citizens stranded in Mexico. You can give it to me when you call."

Silence. "I'm writing this down."

"Good. I'll explain everything later."

"I'm not sure I want to know. It sounds like a mess. How bad is your truck? Can you drive it?"

"Not yet. Another thing: I need the name of a broad-spectrum antibiotic."

"For what? Are you hurt?"

Rugg said it was a cut. "Nothing serious. I want to get ahead of it."

She gave him two names. He recognized one.

"Take 250 mg every eight hours or 500 mg every twelve. Did they give you a tetanus shot?"

"I'll get one."

He heard background sounds, as though she was opening and closing cabinets.

"Where are you exactly?"

"Los Mochis, Sue. You wrote it down. Don't get out the map now."

"Is Rose safe?"

"She'll be fine."

"What does that mean? Is she there?"

"Yes."

"Can I speak to her."

"She's asleep."

"Where."

"In the lobby. When I get the wire …"

"You take care of her, Bob."

"I will."

"You are all she has now."

"I know. Call me after you wire. And go to church. We both need it." Rugg said he had to hang up.

He returned the voting card to Pedro. "The money should be at the telegraph office tomorrow. I will get a call."

"You see, Pedrito," said the old man. "Favors do make good business."

Young Pedro said his shift ended at seven, at which time he was no longer responsible. He told Rugg he could remain in the lobby, but only if he did not bleed on the floor.

"Sit," said the old man. "Sit before you leak. I will wait. The day manager is my nephew. Do you want water?"

He sat and took the glass and drank. The water cold. He found the wadded pill cup from his shirt pocket. The capsules stuck together. He swallowed one and refolded the cup. Pedro brought a stool from behind the desk and set it before Rugg. He laid a folded newspaper on it. "For the drippings."

"Gracias," Rugg said. He elevated his amputated leg.

Pedro stood at the door, looking out. "You should see a doctor, Mr. Rugg."

Rugg said he had come from the Hospital Civil.

"No wonder," Pedro said. He added that quacks and incompetents abounded in the government hospitals.

Rugg said his sister was a nurse.

Pedro said his sister was dead, killed with a machete by her jealous husband after she made him a goat.

"Don't talk about such things," said young Pedro.

The old man grinned. "Pedrito doesn't like the dirty laundry aired outside."

Rugg said nothing.

Later the old man pointed him to the restroom. Inside, Rugg stared in the mirror. Gone from his eyes the way he had gazed past trouble. His face a battered mask of himself. He sat to remove the dressing and to apply the bottled iodine to the wound. He saw no pus on the blooded gauze. After he bandaged the leg, he sat holding his head in his hands, waiting for the medication to dull the pain. He wept without sound. "Take care of her," Sue had said. A supplication his wife had made. "Take care of her, Bob." How the dying entrust love to love's keeping. How the trusted endure. Four years gone. Rose left with her mother's laugh, the mimicked gesture of swiping back her hair. The fragile pout. Left to him its memory, his love for an only child. Sacrifice the sum of nothing if he could not save her.

When a knock rattled the door, Rugg sat up.

"All right in there?" inquired Pedro.

Rugg wiped his eyes on his sleeve before he emerged. He said he had dozed.

5

We park on Tabachines and wait for a bato to drive into the neighborhood. We know his car. Perico sits on the corner watching for him, ready to radio. The job is to lift the bato and take him to El Sin. That's what our crew does. We lift batos. And we boost cars. The cars are for jobs. The batos owe El Sin or he owes them — I don't know more than that. My job is to limp across the street to slow down the bato so our crew can bumper and box him. Even bad batos slow down for a cripple. Perico says I'm a moving speed bump. We call him Perico because he repeats everything he hears, the same as a parrot. I sit in our ride waiting for him to radio when I see a traffic cop roll by tailing a Mercury Marquis. The cop stops the Marquis right in front of us and he gets down to talk to the driver. Our crew boss, Niquelado, says something like, "Who is that son-of-a-violated-mother?" He pulls our ride up to where the cop stands, and he rolls down the glass to ask the cop his business. Niquelado wears his mask. The cop doesn't answer. "You're in the wrong neighborhood," NQ tells him. The cop looks at his feet. "Sorry, boss," he answers. NQ tells him that civilians are watching. "Leave, you fool," he says. That's how NQ talks to traffic cops. The cop leaves. Shortly after, Perico radios that the bato is coming. I get down. When I see his car, I give him a chance to spot me before I limp into the street, exercising my pedestrian right-of-way. The bato slows and stops. NQ and the crew lift him and force him into the back seat of another ride. That's the last time I see him. His ride is left on the street with the keys in it and the engine running. We don't boost old Renaults.

We boost late-model rides — four-door and fast — the kind good for jobs — jobs that aren't my business to know about. What I know is, no one keeps a ride. That's one of El Sin's rules. He has another rule too: We don't boost from women — not because they're women, but because they aren't like men. Men know their ride is gone as soon as they see the masks and guns. They know about insurance. Men aren't in love with a ride enough to throw the keys out the window or to hold tight to the steering wheel to keep from getting pulled out of the seat. That's what women do. Women are macha that way. If they can't have the ride, they don't want anyone to have it.

One of the places we hit are store parking lots. A lot of batos get careless outside a store. Most make the mistake of unlocking their rides before they reach them, showing off their fobs to the poor stiffs who stick a key in the door hole. My job is to hustle a tip from the bato after he unlocks but before he opens the door. I climb up on the hood and wash the glass. I dress shabby and carry a bottle and rag. When I hear the door locks pop, I wait until the bato sees me on the hood before I jump down and limp. "Hey, mister, a little help," I say, or something pathetic like that. The keys are already in his hand. His eyes go to the glass, sometimes to the hood. His mind is on paint scratches, rag streaks, pocket change, but mostly on crippled me standing with my hand stuck in his face. He's a done bato. Our ride pulls up, and the next thing he sees are enough masked men with enough guns to know he's a fool if he doesn't give up the keys. A few batos need a pistol smack for convincing. Like NQ says, guns don't have to shoot to hurt. I climb into our ride fast, not wanting my face to be the last thing the bato sees. I'm the only one not wearing a mask.

Sometimes we boost from used car lots, and once we pulled a double boost from the GMC Chevrolet dealership in

Culiacán. It's a big lot with next year's models. I limp into the showroom with XL, both of us cleaned up. XL pretends he's a customer. I'm his crippled son. XL tells the salesman he's looking to buy a full-size family car, like a Tahoe or a Yukon, in white or silver. The salesman fetches the keys to show us both. We follow him into the lot, where he opens the Tahoe. We climb in, me sucking up the sweet new car smell. It's got leather seats. I'm supposed to keep my mouth shut, so when the salesman asks me if I like it, I just nod. Then XL lets him unlock the Yukon. We don't even get in. When XL says, "I'll take both," the salesman laughs. No joke is too dumb for a car salesman, but his laughing stops as soon as he sees himself surrounded by Indians with no cavalry in sight. To his credit, he is quick to cooperate — life first, screw the cars. Our crew drives the new rides off the lot. After running a few blocks, we stop to let Terre get down to check the wheels for road locks and to disconnect the tracking boxes. He worked in a tire shop as a kid, and then for a mechanic.

XL has his own story, one I hear from Perico, who, like I said, repeats everything he hears. After a shoot-out with the Bátiz brothers, XL bled out so much that the Red Cross medics called him dead on the scene and sent him to the morgue instead of the hospital. El Sin took a crew to lift the body from the morgue and to deliver it to the family to have a burial where the relatives of the Bátiz brothers wouldn't show up. El Sin and XL are cousins. When the crew hits the morgue, they find XL on the floor in a back room with the garbage cans, his body thrown out like it was a dead dog left for the trash. He's lying face down and bleeding into the floor drain. The flies have found him, and the thing is, XL is warm when they pick him up. He's not stiff like a dead bato. Someone tells El Sin, and what happens next is, El Sin shoots the guy in charge of the morgue. Shoots him, but not dead. Then El Sin has the crew drag the bato into the same back room. They leave him facedown to bleed into the floor drain. XL is taken to a clinic where El Sin knows the doctor and the doctor knows how to fix bullet holes without remembering he fixed them. As for the Bátiz brothers, XL got them both before he went down, this, according to Perico, who says El Sin followed up by killing their mother on the last day of the novena for her dead sons, letting the woman pray for their journey before he sent her on her own. I listen and keep my mouth shut. Perico says he's run with El Sin and XL since the days when they fought side by side as soldiers in the sierra, shooting it out on the government side against dope growers and trafficking delinquents. He says they shot a lot of growers and donkeys, and they burned a lot of ranches and dope fields, but there was no end to it, and none of them wanted to stay in the soldiering business, even though they made good money, especially El Sin, who was a lieutenant. Perico says they still dress in their uniforms for jobs where they want to look like soldiers — to snatch a bato at a roadblock or to get into a police station. Like I said, I listen and keep my mouth shut.

The next time I see the scar-faced Zuky, he's in an Escalade we boosted days before, and he's chauffeuring El Sin. They pull up to our ride, and I hear Zuky ask our driver, "You got Rayo?" Our driver rolls down the back glass, and there I am. "Get in, dumbass," Zuky tells me. It's only the three of us in the Escalade, me riding in the back. On the dash in front of El Sin lays a pistol with silver grips. El Sin asks me if I've shot a gun before. He doesn't turn around to look at me. I tell him no, that I haven't gotten the chance. He nods and asks me if I went to school, and I say I went as far as sixth grade. "Did you fail or drop out?" he asks. "Both," I say. Then he asks me how I hurt my foot, and I tell him. He doesn't laugh. Zuky did, but not El Sin. He just nods. What he asks next sounds like a trick question. He asks if I have ever stolen anything from someone who trusted me. I think about it. I've stolen a lot of things from a lot of people, mostly strangers. I stole money from my stepdaddy before he ran me off. I stole pocket change from my aunt when I got the chance. Because neither of them ever trusted me, they don't consider in my answer.

When I think about it, I can't name a person who trusts me, not one, so that's what I tell him. El Sin nods again. Then he turns around and looks at me. "I want to trust you," he says. It's the closest I've seen El Sin. He has an easy face to look at, no meanness there. Not like Zuky. His lips go thin when he smiles and his eyes shine. I don't know what to say. I want to take it as a compliment, but I know it's probably a warning in disguise — "I want to trust you, but don't steal from me." Smart people say stuff without having to spell it out, and El Sin is smart. "Thanks," I say, which is all that comes to me. We ride to a bus stop where Zuky tells me to get down and watch for a bato who wears glasses and carries a briefcase. He gives me a phone. "Call when he gets off the bus."

I wait across the street from the stop, watching the passengers get off the route buses. I wonder if Zuky has moved up or down the ladder, chauffeuring for El Sin. Later I spot the bato getting off the bus. I make the call, and when the Escalade pulls up, I get in and direct them to where the bato walks. He's in no hurry, and we catch up and curb him. The silver gun still sits on the dash. El Sin rolls down his window and says, "Professor, may we speak, please?" That's when I learn the bato is a teacher. He stops and looks at El Sin. "Do I know you?" he asks. El Sin says, "Not personally, but you know my nephew, Archivaldo, one of your students." The teacher's face goes crooked, like he bit a lime. "Ah yes," he says, sounding serious. El Sin offers him a ride, and Zuky unlocks the doors, but the profe doesn't move. He says he doesn't want to occasion an inconvenience, which is fancy teacher talk for no. El Sin tells him it's no trouble. The profe says he isn't going far, just around the corner. I watch him from behind the tinted glass. The profe looks nervous. El Sin says, "Please, I insist. We can talk about my nephew while we ride. He's a good boy. He wants to stay in your school." The profe tries to smile, but the sour taste isn't letting him. He thanks El Sin with a double gracias. "I must walk for the exercise," he says. His eyes say more — they've seen the gun on the dashboard. He steps back from the curb. El Sin's voice stays friendly. "Profe, please. We do not want this to cause friction." The word is new to me. The other thing that's new is the news that El Sin has a nephew. Uncle El Sin sounds weird. The profe says, "I know what you want, but that is impossible. The paperwork is done. He is out." I watch El Sin nod. He says, "Anything is possible, Profe. The paperwork can be undone. You are the school director." The profe says he won't do it, and I see El Sin reach for the gun. He pulls back the slide to load it. I'm guessing the teacher just failed the exam. Then my window suddenly rolls down, and I'm looking at him, and he at me, no *tinted glass between us. El Sin turns around and hands me the gun. "Shoot him when I tell you," he says, loud enough for the profe to hear.*

Like I told El Sin, I've never shot a gun before — not at a window, not at a dog — but it's not my first time holding one. Nacho lets me play with his Ruger, which he showed me how to load and where to unlock the safety. El Sin's pistol feels heavier. I grip it and point it one-handed. The teacher is close enough that I don't need to aim. Any shot out the window hits him. I watch his eyes find mine, but he doesn't speak. El Sin says, "This is what I'm trying to prevent, Profe — what you see here — a boy with a gun. Do you want my nephew to become another boy with a gun? I don't think so. This boy here will not pull the trigger unless I tell him. But I cannot speak for my nephew. We do not want that, do we? It is bad for you and bad for him. What I want is to keep him in school. You are a teacher. You should want this too. It is the best way for a boy to grow up. Am I wrong?" It's a long speech, but I'm not falling asleep. I check to make sure the safety is off, and then I stare at a stain on the profe's shirt. That's where I'll shoot. I don't think about anything else, not whether it's right or wrong, not whether this bato lives or dies, not about what happens after. I'm in the circle and I'm holding

El Sin's gun. My mind is mostly on my finger, though my eyes are on the profe. He doesn't look afraid — more like he wants to throw up. "It makes no difference," he says. "Your nephew will become the boy you speak of, even if he stays in school. He will become this boy here." The profe points at me. I don't like pointing fingers. My limp fetches enough. El Sin says, "Perhaps. But we must give him the opportunity that this boy didn't have. It is only fair. This boy has no one to litigate on his behalf." I have no idea what that means, but I know I'm still part of the conversation. For the first time the profe smiles. It's barely a smile. "Litigate? Is that what you call this?" he says. I'm thinking he and El Sin have connected over the big words, but then El Sin's voice gets chippy. "Call it your last chance," he says. "Today I ask you for a favor. Tomorrow I ask your replacement. Do you want to give me his name before you are replaced?"

Zuky hasn't spoken since we stopped, which is a long silence for him. His eyes check the street. I wonder what this Archivaldo kid did to get thrown out of school and leave the director with a pistol pointed at his shirt stain. "Fine," the profe says. "What choice do you people give anyone? I will do the paperwork. But tell him he must attend class. To stay in school, he must go to school." I'm guessing Archivaldo is lazy, like I was. El Sin says, "He will be in your office tomorrow, Profe. Thank you for reconsidering. I'm in your debt. You may go."

My window rolls up. Zuky hits the gas. "What a whoreson-of-a-goat," he says. El Sin says nothing. He turns around. When I start to hand him the gun, he tells me to keep it. "Practice," he says. I want to ask him if it's loaded, but I don't. I figure it's enough to know he trusted me with the gun, trusted me to pull the trigger on his word. Zuky looks at me in the mirror. "Don't shoot off your good foot, dumbass." Later, when I'm by myself, I check the pistol, and sure enough it's loaded. The grips have an eagle and snake drawn in the silver. Like the flag.

RUGG AWOKE IN the lobby chair, the hotel daylit. Pedro appeared, bringing a Styrofoam cup with hot water and a jar of Nescafé. Inside the jar a plastic spoon. "Your leg stopped leaking, Mr. Rugg." He pointed to the newspaper where Rugg's leg rested on the stool. The paper without bloodstains.

After Rugg mixed his coffee, he handed back the jar. Instant coffee the best joe for trouble, his father liked to say.

"Carlos is my nephew," Pedro said, introducing the tall youth who manned the desk. "His father is my brother, the owner."

Rugg nodded, then drank the coffee. He asked Pedro if he owned a car.

The old man shook his head. When Rugg asked him if he could drive, Pedro looked surprised. "Absolutely I drive, Mr. Rugg. I was a bus driver on interstate routes for eighteen years."

"Uncle, you have no license," Carlos interjected.

The old man waved off the reminder. He said driving with or without a license was still driving.

"I need a car," Rugg said, "and a driver."

Pedro touched his chest. "At your orders."

Rugg finished the coffee. The old man turned to his nephew. "Carlos, ask your wife to borrow the car," he said.

"No," the nephew answered.

Rugg said he would need the car for days, possibly weeks. "I will buy one."

"Carlos, ask your wife if she sells her car," Pedro said.

"Forget it," the nephew replied.

The old man said there were many cars on the lots, not all of them reliable. "But why do you buy a car, Mr. Rugg? When your leg is better, you can take a bus or a plane."

Rugg said he needed to find his stolen truck.

Pedro shook his head. "Maybe you should let them keep it."

"I can't," Rugg said.

"It must be a good truck."

Rugg nodded. "It is my only truck. I want it back."

The old man said he was willing to drive Rugg anywhere, except into the mouths of wolves.

"My uncle is not supposed to drive," Carlos said. "He had an accident."

Pedro looked at his nephew. "Mr. Rugg is in a tight spot with one foot. Don't be like Pedrito, saying no to everything. The accident was years ago. My driving is good." He took Rugg's empty cup and told Carlos to order breakfast tacos for Mr. Rugg. "Call Zurdo's. Order six."

"Are you buying, Uncle?"

"No, take it from the box. Mr. Rugg will reimburse us when he receives his money. Right, Mr. Rugg?"

Rugg nodded. He knew he would not eat six tacos.

Beyond the lobby's windowed front, traffic in the street. Rugg watched the vehicles pass. What was the chance, he thought, the chance that he would spot her out the window, her fair hair glimpsed? No chance. Finding Pedro the only luck so far. Cocksure but not stupid. He would figure out this was not about a truck.

The boy who delivered the tacos wore flip-flops and drove a moped with a food box mounted on the rack. He carried the order to the front desk, his eyes on Rugg's elevated leg. "What happened to that guy?" he asked. The old man said, "Did we order tacos or a nosy boy on a bike?" When the boy left, Pedro told Rugg delivery boys were employed by gangsters to watch neighborhoods and spy on hotels. "These boys circle like falcons."

"Not all boys," said the nephew.

"Did I say all, Carlos? Ask your father. They watched him coming and going until they bled him. Why do think I'm here?"

The tacos deep-fried and filled with marinated pork. Rugg ate two off a plastic plate. "There's more," Pedro offered, his mouth full. Rugg told the old man to finish them.

When the sound of guests descended from the rooms, he left the lobby and stood outside, the day warm. A middle-aged couple without luggage emerged from the hotel and set off separately down the street. Speaker music blared from a nearby beer store. Rugg looked for a name on the hotel but saw only the neon sign that tersely billed lodging. He surveyed the block in both directions, eyeing the transit of vehicles, the drivers, the occupants. He saw no police. His plan a plan still in the making — to search for Rose without the cops, the old man driving. Then what, he did not know. Already two weeks gone. No photo to show. No edge gained on these villains, except his apparent death. No way to know how far they would take her, though what they could do to her a prospect that tainted his every thought. When he felt the pain rise in his leg, he reentered the lobby. He asked Pedro for water to take the last of the capsules from the pill cup. Then he sat and elevated his leg, the dressing freshly bled.

His sister called in the afternoon. He heard the nephew answer. Rugg crutched to the desk and took the phone. "Sue?"

"I had trouble getting through. You didn't give me the hotel name."

"It's fine. You got through."

She read the confirmation for the wire. Rugg wrote it on a registration card the nephew handed him. When he asked for the consulate number, she gave it to him.

"Now can you tell me what happened, Bob?"

He knew that some of the truth had to be shared — should they not return. "We were carjacked, Sue. I was shot. That's it. I'm buying a car to drive us to the consulate."

"Shot? Didn't you say it was an accident?"

"I did. The details don't matter. As soon as we get the passports, we'll head north. I need you to send me copies of our birth certificates and our photo IDs. In my desk …"

"Damn it, Bob! The details? Where were you shot?"

"The leg. It's fine. In the center drawer is my pilot's license. The birth certificates are in a folder in the file drawer. Rose left her school ID in her room or in the pink backpack. She's not sure."

"OK."

"I need color. You can scan and email them from my computer." He gave her the password.

"What about the police? You are a gunshot victim. Have you reported it?" The emergency room nurse talking.

Rugg said the police were investigating. "It's different here. Slower."

"Is she awake?"

"Who?"

"Rose! Who else?"

Rugg fought back the desperation. "She's in the room. I'm in the lobby."

"What time is it there?"

He read the time off the wall clock.

"Can I speak to her?"

"There's no room phone, Sue. I'll have her call when we get to a regular hotel. I promise. Send that email please. I'll find a computer."

Silence.

Rugg said he had to go. "They need the phone. We'll talk soon."

He hung up, his breath held. If she didn't hear from him again, she would know. So traveled no news from distant places.

On a second registration card he wrote the wire information, adding Sue's name and telephone. He showed Carlos the consulate number. "Tollfree," he explained.

The man who picked up answered in Spanish. When Rugg gave his name and identified himself as an American citizen, the man switched to English. "I'm a duty officer. How may I help?" Rugg remembered how the silver-haired gavillero boss had moved seamlessly between the idioms of his men and his victims. That graveled voice.

Rugg told the duty officer his story, detailing their departure from Nogales, the gunmen, the carjacking, the abduction of Rose, his injury, the passports, his predicament. The officer listened until Rugg finished. "Have you been detained? Are the police involved?" he asked.

"Not detained," Rugg said. "I have not told the police. I'm not sure what they know. Maybe nothing. I'm inclined to leave it that way for now."

The duty officer asked Rugg for his full name and that of his daughter, their ages, domiciles, occupations, the dates and times of the events, the details of Rugg's injury, the make and model of his truck, and a phone number where he could be reached. Rugg had served as a US Marine in his youth. He knew the information drill, the protocol of forms. When the duty officer asked if he had money, Rugg said he had a wire coming from his sister. The officer asked the sister's name, domicile, occupation, and phone number.

Rugg jumped ahead. "I must find my daughter," he said. "The men who took her have a two-week start. Can you locate her passport?" Rugg knew the RFID chip in passports had a far-field trackability not openly acknowledged. He also knew the chip was the equivalent of a tiny radio station under concrete. To be heard, the passport cover had to be open. The officer said, "We can locate her if she crosses the border or gets on a plane." Rugg asked, "Are you sure?" When the officer replied that the consul could better answer his question tomorrow morning after 9:00 a.m., Rugg said, "OK. How can you help me now? I need direction. Where should I look? What's your intel on road abductions? I can't be the first."

"Again, Mr. Rugg, the consul is looped into that information. What I know is that we can facilitate emergency financial assistance to get you to Hermosillo, where we can authorize a provisional passport. For legal assistance we can provide a list of local attorneys who speak English and, should you need a medical specialist, we can put you in touch with a practitioner in your area. You said you lost your foot. That's a serious injury."

Rugg said he would live, but his daughter might not. "You are the duty officer for emergency calls. This is an emergency. Give me some informed advice."

The officer said his first advice was to stay calm. "Have they contacted you about a ransom?"

Rugg glanced into the handset, as though to glimpse the idiot on the other end. "Ransom? They shot me. They left me for dead. Who are they going to extort? It was a carjacking. My daughter wasn't kidnapped. She was abducted. Who do I contact? Where do I search? What's your blueprint for this? If you don't have one, I want to speak to the person who does."

"Mr. Rugg, I understand you are upset …"

"Pissed is closer."

"… But to expedite your daughter's return we must first assess the situation. I will apprise the consul, and he will call. Will you be available at this number tomorrow?"

"I will be looking for my daughter tomorrow and all the days that follow until I find her."

"OK. How about a cell phone where you can be reached?"

"They took it. Give me his cell and name. I'll call him."

The officer said he wasn't allowed to disclose the cell phone numbers of consulate employees. He apologized. "But you can contact him at our day phone, extension 450. His name is Eric White. Do you have our numbers?"

"Yeah."

"I urge you to call him first thing tomorrow. Where are you staying?"

"I'm calling from a hotel lobby."

"What hotel?"

"It's doesn't matter."

"Mr. Rugg, please. We want to help. Will they take messages?"

Rugg said, "You can try, but I'll be out until I find her or kill these sonofabitches."

Silence from the duty officer.

"I'm hanging up," Rugg advised. "Don't notify the police."

The officer said the consulate strongly recommended against US citizens negotiating directly with members of criminal organizations.

Rugg said, "I won't be negotiating."

"Neither do we condone vigilante justice, Mr. Rugg. As a foreigner in Mexico, you are subject to laws that may not afford you the protections available to an individual in the United States. Your citizenship will not help you avoid arrest or prosecution."

"You'll hear from me," Rugg said before he hung up.

6

The pistol El Sin gives me is a Colt 1911. I have two boxes of 9mm ammunition for it, and the first time I shoot it I'm with Fer and Nacho at a dump site, burning and burying our road business from one of the boosts. Nobody else comes. Nacho says the silver grips make the Colt a lucky gun. He pulls his Ruger from where it's tucked in his pants and holds it with his arm outstretched, looking over the barrel. "Like this," he says. "Only fools don't aim." I do the same with the Colt. Then Fer says, "Shoot the rats." There are plenty to shoot, big ones. They come here because we come here, living off what we dump. I check to see if a round is chambered before I flip the safety, point, and pull the trigger. The rats scatter. I empty the magazine. I love the sound of the pistol crack, but I don't hit a rat. Fer and Nacho laugh themselves to tears. Nacho tells me to reload and shows me how to aim low for the recoil. The rats are gone, but the vultures are back in the trees. Nacho says vultures aren't smart like rats, but they take a bullet like a man. I aim at the nearest one and hit it first shot. It tries to fly before it drops to the ground. I hit two more with six shots. Fer tells me to finish them off, so I reload and walk to the tree, where I try to shoot each of the birds in the head. It's not easy. They flap and lift dust. Their heads are small and their necks move like snakes. Knocking them out of a tree is more fun than killing them. I empty another magazine before they stop moving. Fer and Nacho laugh and cheer. When they point at me, I see vulture blood on my shirt. The spots are black. Nacho says I must shoot smarter before El Sin lets me pull it on a job. "Not all batos run like rats," he says. "Some shoot back."

The Colt is warm and smoky-smelling. My hand sweats from squeezing the grips, and my heart is whipped up. I don't like the bird blood, but the shooting part is large and speedy, though it's harder than it looks. I'm thinking I'll get good at it, but not right away. Meanwhile, I carry the Colt tucked in my pants.

R UGG GAVE PEDRO the card with the telegraph information. A choice made to trust this old man. "Now can I get a room?" he asked.

Pedro told his nephew to give Rugg a room near the stairs, one with air-conditioning. "I guarantee payment." When Carlos wavered, the old man showed him the card. "Do you think Mr. Rugg invented this? Did he invent his leg? Your father wants business. Mr. Rugg will stay while we look for his truck. If you do not give him a room, tomorrow he will turn this paper into money and go to another hotel, a better hotel. Does your father want that?"

The nephew handed Rugg a registration card. Rugg pointed to the one he had filled out, left in a cubicle by young Pedro. The old man took the key and led Rugg up the stairs. "It is good lodging," he said, "for the price."

Low-wattage luminance fell from a pair of sconce fixtures, the room without windows. Above the double bed hung an oval ceiling mirror. Pedro turned on the AC, an old Carrier framed in the wall. He showed Rugg the bathroom. "There's soap and towels," he said. When he asked if Rugg wanted to order dinner, Rugg replied that he wanted to shower and sleep. Pedro said he would be

downstairs. After he left, Rugg wondered if the old man lived in the lobby.

He removed his clothes and laid them on the bed, the room lacking closet or cabinetry. In the bathroom mirror he examined his shoulder and neck. He sat on the toilet to remove the dressing and check his leg. The wound dry and blood-crusted, the zippered stitches risen in relief. Rugg stood in the narrow shower stall with both faucets open, surprised when hot water arrived. The smell of urine on him. Blood and fecal smears. It was his first shower since Tucson, the night before they crossed the border, Rose in the next room with the TV loud. "Do not open the door for anyone," he had enjoined. Then he had made her engage the deadbolt and hang the security chain. *For nothing.*

Rugg lay naked on the bed, the unbandaged leg propped on a towel. He stared at himself in the ceiling mirror, his first full view of the asymmetry that must save her.

Who's in control now? Where's the illusion?

He had shot men in battle. He had watched them fight even as they died. He had ditched aircraft and crash landed — a witness to survivors drowning, to men burned alive. He had held in his arms the only woman he ever loved, her last breath on his face, and not then, and not before, had he considered the outcome of these events to be in his hands. How he had stayed strong — knowing that control was an illusion, his life not one of his own making. But now he hoped it was so. This once.

With the crutch he hit the light switch. He lay staring into the dark, the rattle of the old Carrier loud in the room. Later he slept and dreamed of nothing.

At the hour Rugg heard the knock, daylight seeped between the AC unit and the wall opening.

"Señor Rugg. Teléfono."

Rugg rose and found his pants. At the door Pedro stood with his Dodgers cap turned to the side, his attire otherwise unchanged. Rugg held to the doorframe. The old man stared at his shirtless torso, the wounds and scars.

"Man or woman?" Rugg asked.

"A woman trying to speak Spanish."

Sue.

He told Pedro to tell her he would call back.

Before he descended, Rugg disinfected the wound and dressed it with the last gauze pads. When he exited the room, the door left unlocked.

Young Pedro stood at the desk. He placed on the counter a promissory note for signature. Rugg signed it.

"I showed him the wire number," explained the old man, "but Pedrito is a hard one. Like his mother."

Rugg said he would pay when they returned from the telegraph office. He asked young Pedro to call a taxi.

Outside, the sun unleashed in a cloudless sky. Rugg crutched to the taxi. He rode, taking in the streets, the neighborhood housewives queued to buy tortillas, the crowded breakfast stands with patrons standing to eat. School girls dressed in uniforms waited at bus stops.

Rugg observed them, their laughing faces beyond all tomorrows.

"Your wife is mad at me, I think," Pedro remarked.

Rugg said it was his sister, the nurse, who had called.

"I did my impossible to make her understand, but she said, "No comprendo. ¿Dónde Rosa? Rosa, por favor." I told her there was no Rosa. That's when she sounded mad. I need English for these situations."

"Rose is my daughter," Rugg said.

"Ah." The old man nodded. "That explains it."

Rugg silent. Explanation pending, he thought. The taxi advanced.

"I have no daughter," the old man said. "It's a shame. A daughter takes the father's side. Not a son."

Rugg said he had only Rose.

"A beautiful name."

"Yes."

They rode.

"Are you married, Mr. Rugg?"

Rugg said his wife was dead.

"Oh. I'm sorry to hear it."

When they passed a used car lot, he read the sale prices waxed on the windshields, calculating the dollars needed to buy one. He asked the old man how long a purchased vehicle could circulate on temporary plates.

"Forever," replied Pedro, "if you pay. This is Mexico."

At the telegraph office the taxista bristled when the old man told him the fare wouldn't be paid until they finished their business, which would be after the office opened. "Does this look like a limousine?" the taxista asked.

"Does this look like a man who rides one?" Pedro shot back. "Look at him. He needs money to buy decent crutches and pay you. Show consideration for the maimed."

The taxista parked and waited in his car.

Early arrivals stood queued at the telegraph entrance. The old man went to the front of the line and spoke. "Please spare this mutilated man an exhausting wait on one leg. He will go directly to the handicapped window and not delay you further."

Customers stepped aside, allowing Rugg to advance. He observed the telegraph office hours on the glass front. When the doors opened, the old man followed him inside and strode to the teller on duty, presenting the card with the wire information. Rugg saw no window for the handicapped.

The teller studied Pedro's voting card before he glanced at Rugg. "Is this money for you?" he asked the old man.

Pedro pointed to the card. "Whose picture is that? Who has the particulars? Do I look like Juárez on a horse?" When the teller said he would need to get a supervisor to authorize the amount, the old man said, "Give it to me in big bills. My pockets are small."

Rugg expected further interrogation, possibly trouble, but the teller returned shortly with a cashbox. He removed two bundles of banknotes, broke the currency straps, and counted the bills. When he finished, he rebundled the money. "Sign here," he said, passing the receipt under the transaction window. His eyes avoided Rugg. After Pedro signed, the teller pushed the bundles beneath the glass.

The old man removed one bill from the bundles before he tucked them under his shirtfront. Back in the taxi he showed the bill to the driver. "We are men of good faith," he said. He handed Rugg the receipt but kept the bundled money under his shirt. Rugg told the driver to take them to a pharmacy and a medical supply store. He said they would pay for his time.

At the pharmacy he crutched the aisles, the old man in tow. Rugg handed him rolls of gauze, packages of compression bandages, safety pins, a bottle of hydrogen peroxide, nail scissors, thumb forceps, a shaving kit, toothpaste, and a toothbrush. At the counter he asked the female attendant for oral penicillin and a strong pain medication. The attendant did not request a doctor's prescription. She set before him a box of Amoxicilina and a bottle of hydrocodone tablets. When Rugg asked if there was someone who could administer a tetanus shot, the woman led him to the rear of the pharmacy, where she removed an ampule from a refrigerator and prepared a disposable syringe. Rugg sat in a chair while she disinfected his arm and injected the toxoid. At the counter she rang up the items. Pedro paid and carried the bagged items to the taxi.

Rugg ate without appetite at the menudo stand the old man picked for breakfast while they waited for the medical supply store to open. They sat among men on stools, sipping the bowls of steamy broth. Rugg took the medications, noting the time on the watch of a fellow diner. In the supply store he tested the crutches before he chose one with aluminum frames and adjustable handgrips. Rugg left the store on the new crutches, leaving the stolen ones with the clerk.

The taxi drove them to an outdoor clothing bazaar, where Rugg purchased shirts, two pairs of wide-legged jeans, undergarments, a belt, a cheap wallet, and boot socks. At a cap stall he picked an off-green snapback, the front without letters or logo — a cap to minify a big gringo. They were returning to the taxi when a well-dressed man wearing wristwatches on his forearm approached Rugg. "Tengo Rolex," he said. Rugg regarded the watches. "Stolen?" he asked. The vendor protested. "No sir. These watches were pawned and unclaimed. I have papers." Rugg followed him to a stand, where he inspected the timepieces displayed in the glass cabinets. He did not see his Breitling, or any pilot watch, but he saw many quality pieces once worn by other men. He chose an analog Timex with a leather strap.

On their return to the hotel Rugg asked the old man what ambulance service brought accident victims from the highway to the hospitals.

"The Red Cross," he answered.

The taxista pointed to a Red Cross donation sticker on his windshield. "I give annually," he said.

At the hotel the old man dickered with the driver over the fare before he followed Rugg inside with the purchases.

Carlos stood behind the desk. "You have phone messages," he reported. "Mr. White from the consulate. And your sister. I didn't understand her." Rugg told Carlos that he would not take any calls. Then he asked for a room with no mirror on the ceiling, one distant from the stairs with a view of the street.

"Air-conditioning?" Carlos asked.

Rugg said it didn't matter.

The second room with a wooden sash window and no air-conditioner in the wall. Inside, Pedro gave Rugg the bundles of money. Rugg counted out five thousand pesos and handed it to the old man, telling him to consider it payment for services, past and future.

"No, it is too much," Pedro protested.

Rugg said it was small money for his many favors. Then he asked if the hotel had a safe where he could leave part of the cash. The old man said the hotel had a lockable security box that could be stolen by a blind man. "Keep the money with you," he advised. Rugg went to the window and surveyed the street. It was a corner room furnished with a nightstand and chair, the window fitted with a vintage roller shade attached to a pull string. Rugg raised the shade and lowered it, remembering when, as a boy, he had tied a balsa glider to such a pull-down string before he sprang the shade, letting the ratchet and gravity pawl mechanism lift the balsa in the air. His first flight.

While the old man waited downstairs, Rugg changed out of the clothes the woman had given him. He folded them and set them on a chair, as the woman had done. How far this attire had taken him a gift beyond measure. He cleansed the wound with the peroxide and redressed it, the bandage bloodied, the sutured flaps of flesh not yet knitted. At times Rugg felt the foot as though it were there. He felt it tingle and turn hot, then cold. Sometimes it itched.

With the scissors he cut the spandex tops off two boot socks and pulled the opening of the first sock over the stump as far as the heel turn, leaving the toe wedge to dangle. The second sock he pulled over the first. The jeans rode wide enough for Rugg to double the empty pantleg and pin it above the knee. The shirt collar covered his neck wound. He adjusted the crutches' handgrips and circled the bed, trying not to hunch. He lifted the window shade and checked the street. The hotel entrance visible. It was a good room.

In the lobby he paid Carlos for the night owed and for an additional week's lodging. He settled up for the delivered food.

It was noon when they took a taxi to the Movistar store, where Rugg purchased a mobile phone and multiple calling cards. As the old man stood by, he loaded the mobile and dialed Rose's number, prefixing the country code. The call went to an automated message stating that the number was no longer in service. He hung up and dialed again. After the second try, Rugg closed the mobile and dialed his old number, listening to the same automated message.

They visited three auto lots before he found the truck he wanted, a Ford Ranger with an automatic transmission and an extended cab. White. No markings. A Mazda dressed in Detroit. The old man test-drove it, Rugg measuring his traffic IQ and eyesight from the passenger seat. That he had driven a bus for a large part of his life was evident by how he hugged the shoulder. Otherwise, he freewheeled.

Rugg told the salesman to invoice the truck to Pedro. When the paperwork was completed, they drove to the Pemex station, where the old man got down to check the oil and tire pressure and to wave away a window wipe who approached the hood. Rugg set the correct time on the truck's dash clock. After they gassed up, Pedro asked, "Which way, Mr. Rugg?"

He told the old man to take Highway 15 north to the Sonoran state line, where they had stolen his truck.

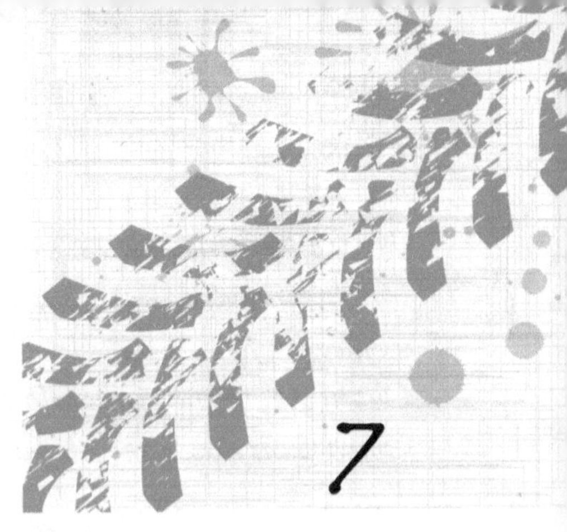

7

I want Cachoro's job — driving a crew. It's a good job, chasing down the boosts, boxing and curbing and bumping a ride if a bato doesn't pull over. I don't know how to drive yet, but I will. My bad foot gives me the itch to put my good foot on the gas and bring some truth to why people call me Speedy.

When XL puts me on a highway crew, I run in the scout car, which trolls the road to spot new boosts. Sometimes we park off the asphalt to better check the rides that pass. If the highway has a pull-off lane, we might stop, lift the hood, and pretend a breakdown. Other times we drive under the speed limit and let the rides pass us until one goes by that we want. We don't look dangerous. We look invisible. Two of us spot from the scout car, watching for club cab trucks and the big passenger rides and any of the fast sport wagons. We only mark the out-of-state rides and those with gringo plates. I can read the makes and models from my juggling days, but at night it's not so easy, when a ride goes by flat-out. That's why two of us watch before Chango keys the Motorola to turn loose the chase cars, which wait down the highway.

I scout a lot of boosts before XL tells me to run with Cachoro and the chasers. Cachoro took over for RollsRoyce, who died for nothing, according to Perico. Rolls had walked away from flipped rides and head-on crashes, but it was a drunk old lady that killed him. She T-boned his Crown Victoria as he backed out of a Chinese restaurant on a full stomach, knocking the fried rice out of him — exact words from Perico, who saw him dead and says there wasn't a scratch on him. That's when Cachoro became the lead driver. I ride back seat middle, and I unload with the crew when the boost is curbed. The guy riding shotgun goes for the driver. The second guy out hits the passenger side. Others do road cover and backup. My job is to move on the batos once they're commanded. I lift wallets and frisk for pocket knives and pistols, but I don't take jewelry or watches. Those are orders. I wear a mask, which I like. The Colt is on me, but I can't use it. After the boost is ours, I go with the crew that cleans it at the dump site. When I'm not on a job, I stay at the crash house, unless Zuky sends me to do lookouts in the city. Then I crash with my aunt. None of the crew knows about my aunt, and I know nothing about their aunts, if they have any.

Sometimes El Sin runs with us when we troll the highway. The thing about El Sin is, he doesn't wear a mask and he always talks to the batos. If there is a girl in the ride, he has her lifted, but only if she is young and pretty. He leaves the old and fat ones stranded. The other thing about El Sin is, he speaks English. I don't understand it, but I've heard him go on some serious palavers with the tourists, like he has a gringo inside him. Perico says El Sin learned the lingo growing up in Matamoros, where his mother cleaned houses for rich folks, and later, when he lived in Texas, training with the gringo soldiers to fight the dope growers and the trafficking delinquents. Perico says El Sin is no ordinary boss.

I see it firsthand one afternoon when we stop at a red light on the Centenario in a late-model Explorer Sport Trac that we boosted from Sonora. Zuky drives and El Sin rides shotgun. I sit in the rear with Labios. The Centenario is a three-lane boulevard, and we idle in the middle lane, waiting for the light to change. I see El Sin check his mirror. "Hold it," he says to Zuky when the light turns green. The cars in the other lanes roll, but we sit at the green light while traffic backs up behind us. "Is she alone?" El Sin asks. Zuky checks the rearview before he nods. I turn around and see a woman at the wheel of the car on our tail. Labios turns and licks his lips. We call him Labios because whenever he sees a woman, he licks his lips. He can't help it. Perico says women run from him because he looks like he's going to eat them. Our Sport Trac sits at the light. It's a first for me — stopped at a green. Traffic flies by in the other lanes. Batos honk when they drive past, but the woman behind us doesn't hit the horn. El Sin turns to Zuky and says, "What do you bet she doesn't honk?" Zuky grins and answers, "A thousand she honks on the next green." El Sin nods and says, "But you must do her if she honks." Zuky pulls his Glock from his belt and lays it on the seat beside him. "Done," he agrees. The light turns red again. Zuky shifts the truck into Park and he turns down the radio. When the light turns green the second time, we sit there, letting our lane back up. Horn honking starts again, but the woman behind us doesn't hit the hooter. El Sin stares ahead. Zuky grins. "Come on, darling," he says. He picks up the Glock. One driver shouts, "Pendejos!" as he drives by — an insult that would have cost him on any other day, but today Labios laughs. Zuky begs her to honk. The light turns yellow, then red. "Fornication of a woman," Zuky growls. I can tell he wants to do her because she didn't honk. He sets the Glock on the seat and reaches into his pocket and pulls out his wad, peeling off two five-hundreds. El Sin smiles. He tells Zuky to hand them to me. Zuky throws them into the back seat and says, "Here's for doing nothing, dumbass." I pick up the bills. El Sin says, "Rayo, take the money to the driver behind us. Tell her this is her lucky day." Labios opens the door and I get out and limp around to her side of the car. It's a beat-up Caribe with no front plate. I tap her window and motion for her to roll it down, which she does. She may have thought I was a street beggar, until I poke the two five-hundreds through the window. "That's yours," I say. She's young and she wears a nurse's uniform. She looks surprised when she sees the money, but her face goes serious after she sees the Colt stuck in my waist. "There was a bet," I say, pointing to our Explorer. "A bet that you'd honk. But you didn't." She stares at me. I can tell she doesn't get it, so I say, "If you had honked, Zuky would have shot you. But you didn't, so the money is yours. El Sin says to tell you that this is your lucky day." I want to ask her if the horn is broken, but I don't. I return to our ride. Labios is looking back, licking his lips. When the light turns green, Zuky hits the gas. How El Sin knew she wouldn't honk, I couldn't figure. Like Perico says, El Sin is special. Still, it was good to see the scar-faced Zuky lose. Some people are born lucky. Others, not so much.

WHEN RUGG FLEW FOR the Forest Service, he spotted lost ground crews by looking where the conflagrant forests gave them up. Men might hide from each other, but not from the land that confined them, much less one where no man belonged. So Rugg surveilled the road as the old man drove, his pilot's gaze cast to what the towns and the desert gave up that didn't belong.

They left the Carrizo Valley and crossed the state line into Sonora, passing a checkpoint where a uniformed inspector stopped them to search the truck bed before waving them ahead. When Rugg asked the old man if all vehicles crossing the state line were stopped at the checkpoint, Pedro said it was reasonable to expect that every vehicle would be stopped, but, all the same and be that as it may, not all vehicles were stopped.

Rugg rode with his amputated leg propped on a crutch wedged between the passenger seat and the console. He listened to the old man recount the days he ran ten-wheel passenger buses to Tijuana, driving the sinuous and snowbound Rumorosa highway across the Sierra de Juárez. When Rugg inquired about the accident mentioned by the nephew, Pedro replied, "I fell asleep and drove a busload of Christians into a ditch. None were killed, but some were carted off. The state revoked my license. It was bad luck that could have been worse." Rugg said most bad things didn't look so bad until worse things happened. The old man nodded. "My brother says bad luck loves worse luck."

The hum of the tires filled the truck cab. The window wind loud. "Your brother understands luck," Rugg said.

"He should. He had it, then lost it. His money too. And his fat belly."

"This is the brother who owns the hotel?" Rugg asked.

"The same. Since the shakedown, he doesn't show his face. He came every morning, like the newspaper, until one day they were waiting in the lobby. That's what they do. They watch and wait."

Rugg did not know the word for racketeer. "¿Extorcionista?" he suggested.

Pedro nodded and touched underneath his eye to signal vigilance. "My brother was afraid for Carlos. They told him if he didn't pay, they would make Carlos disappear. He paid. Now I stay at the hotel and see to his business. I took down the big sign. It had his name — San Carlos. I brought Pedrito to work nights, so Carlos can be with his wife. We are not as busy as before. Mostly fornicators rent our rooms. The gangsters forgot us."

Rugg told Pedro that his brother had made the only choice a father could make.

At the tollplaza in Estación Don he directed the old man to double back onto the southbound lanes. Rugg remembered the plaza and its attendant, a woman with red-painted nails and drugstore makeup who had smiled at him in a way Rose had noticed. "Did you see that, Dad?" she had asked. "That woman looked at you funny."

"I didn't notice," he had lied.

Then Rose had asked him if he missed her mother. Rugg had said, "Every day. Every hour."

"Don't marry anyone until I grow up and move away. So it's just us at the house. OK?"

"OK," he had said.

The old man stopped at the tollplaza to use the restroom. Rugg remained in the truck, observing a black-and-white Federal Police cruiser parked in the plaza. Inside the cruiser the cops wore sunglasses. Rugg watched them monitor traffic. No vehicle escaped their notice. Every driver's face revealed when the windows came down, the toll paid. It was a good spot to reconnoiter, Rugg decided, and he wondered if the gavilleros had scouted his truck from here. He did not recall seeing a police cruiser parked in the plaza when he and Rose had passed. Red-painted nails and a fetching smile had stolen the moment.

He noted the call number on the cruiser's hood, and he asked the old man if the Federal Police had jurisdiction in the towns and ranches off the highway.

"They go wherever they want," he replied. "They are prepotent crooks without shame."

When they departed south, Rugg checked his watch. One hour he calculated to be the time he and Rose had traveled from the plaza to where the white Cheyenne had stopped them. He eyed the kilometer signposts that sided the highway, unable to recall the last number seen before the assault — no reason to mark it then.

Nothing before him looked familiar. The highway without curves, the desert without landmark. He spotted numerous dirt roads that broke from the thornscrub onto the highway. He observed crossovers in the median strip concealed by tall buffelgrass. There were many places to lurk. He recalled how the Cheyenne had appeared beside him without apparent pursuit, and he recalled the narrow shoulder and the range fence and how it stood clear of scrub where cattle had trampled and grazed. Scrub two weeks grown now.

"What are we looking for?" Pedro asked.

Rugg said he wasn't sure.

The blacktop streaked with the vulcanized burns of hotly weighted tires. The centerline faded. At signpost 85 the fence opened from the highway to accommodate a ditched slope.

"We won't find your truck here," the old man opined.

Rugg nodded. He pressed the emergency flasher on the dash. "Slow down," he said.

He followed the barbed wire that topped the livestock mesh. Where he saw the wires inflected, he told the old man to pull over and stop. Rugg surveyed the road and the embankment, reckoning the spot where he had brought the Ford to a stop. He took in the desert, no cell tower in sight. When he removed the mobile phone from his pocket, he saw the signal bar shrunk. He dialed her number and listened before he pocketed the mobile and descended to crutch the unpaved shoulder. Somewhere here he had stood begging for her life. Here where he had glimpsed her sunlit hair. A place like no other, and now just a place, the violence departed. How crime left its scene to take up new tragedy elsewhere.

He retraced the shoulder, scanning the grass-grown embankment. "Is it something you dropped?" Pedro asked. Rugg used his crutch tip to sweep the grass and kick out a brass casing.

The old man picked it up. "Was this one that got you?"

Rugg took it and read the headstamp. "Maybe," he said, recognizing the round as a 9mm Parabellum shot from a pistol caliber carbine. He had seen only one gavillero carrying such a weapon — the man who had broken his jaw. His narcotic stare and bad teeth stuck in Rugg's head.

Pedro kicked the grass, bending to harvest a handful of .223 Remington casings of the kind fired from an AR-15 or variant. Rugg examined them before he put them in his pocket. He surveyed the scrub brush beyond the fence. The thicket with better cover than he remembered.

He crutched a traverse descent down the embankment and stood studying the fenceline where they had muscled him over the wire, the barbed strands bowed. When he asked the old man if he could cross to the other side and search the ground, Pedro replied, "I'm not so old I can't climb a fence. What do I look for?" Rugg said anything fallen from a man or from his pockets — watch, ring, coins, wrappers, cigarettes. He pointed to the spot where he had punched the gavillero.

The old man circled, kicking the dirt. "Nada," he reported.

Rugg looked off the fenceline in the direction he had fled. "My shoe is out there," he remarked. The old man followed his gaze. "You want me to fetch it?"

"No, it's my left shoe."

He ascended the embankment in a slow zigzag. His leg throbbed. When they stood by the truck, Rugg took in the solitary expanse. A good stretch for carjacking, he reflected. Every hawk his habitat.

A tractor trailer approached and passed them, the bow wave of wind buffeting the Ranger. Rugg followed the truck's retreat, recalling the driver who had stopped his rig on the highway before resuming passage, the road his savior.

Pedro pointed to the spent casings in Rugg's pocket. "Do you think you'll find your truck with those?"

Rugg said it was unlikely. "They are common casings. The most common for killing."

"You know something about guns, Mr. Rugg?"

"I do," Rugg said.

"Were you a cop?"

"Soldier," Rugg answered. "In my youth."

"Ah." The old man looked impressed. "Is that where you got those scars I saw?"

"A few," Rugg admitted. "Others later."

The old man said that too many scars were a sign that a man was running out of places to heal. "These thieves took your foot. What else will they take if you come for your truck?"

Rugg said he was prepared for that.

"It is but my opinion," Pedro added. "Every man knows what he can live without. I think a truck is one such thing."

Rugg stared at the highway centerline where the gavilleros had held him at gunpoint, where the masked boy had taken his wallet but not his watch — the value of what Rugg wore worth less to them than what identified him. How thieves with organization operated. Rules and ruthlessness the mandate. What remained unclear to him was why they would take a teenage girl if only the truck was wanted. And why not let the father live to ransom the daughter? Unless the daughter was not wanted for ransom. "Worth what?" the silver-haired boss had asked when Rugg had offered himself in trade. "You are not as pretty," he had joked, as though he knew her price. The price of prettiness.

He spat on the blacktop, remembering how the boy had winked, taking him into their conspiracy. He knew Rugg would die.

"Mr. Rugg, you have no need for your old truck. You have this one."

Rugg told Pedro that the Ranger would be his to keep once their business was finished.

"No, no, Mr. Rugg. If your desire is to leave Mexico in a truck, then you should leave in this one."

Rugg said that was not the plan. He said he had come to Mexico with his daughter and his plan was to leave with her.

"What? Your daughter?"

Then Rugg told the old man about Rose, the story of her abduction and how the truck meant nothing.

The old man stared. "Those sons-of-a-fornication!" he exclaimed. "Those filthy offspring of the grand raped whore."

Rugg said he needed his help. He said he had told only one other person about Rose. For now, he wanted no one else to know.

Pedro nodded. "I swear on my mother's grave."

"OK."

"Those double whoremothers. That is why your sister asked for Rosa."

Rugg said he had not told his sister, but she suspected something was wrong.

"Sisters are tricky."

"I told the man from the consulate."

Pedro frowned. "Will he call the police?"

Rugg said the man had been told not to, but that didn't mean anything. He said that if the police knew of the carjacking, they had likely been informed by whoever had found him in the desert after the truck and Rose were taken. "I was brought to the hospital without a name — a gunshot gringo from the highway. The police did not come."

The old man nodded. "So the gavilleros think you are dead?"

"Yes."

Pedro said that was a good problem and a bad problem. "To be dead may help you find her. To be a gringo with one foot will help them find you."

"Maybe." He said that without knowing where to look for Rose, he could think of no better way to find her than to first find his truck, and then find the men who took it.

The old man stared at the highway traffic. "How old is Rose? Not too old, I hope."

When Rugg told him, Pedro clucked his teeth.

Rugg knew what the old man thought.

"We need to look in many places, Mr. Rugg. No girl is safe from men here, no matter where she is kept."

Rugg said nothing.

"But your idea is good. We will look for the truck in the highway towns. Maybe they still drive it. If they are dumb enough to keep the truck, they may have your daughter."

There was another option Rugg forced himself to consider — what criminals do with an abducted girl not held for ransom. "Is it possible they would sell her?" he asked.

The old man blinked, his face seeking translation. "You mean sell her to someone?"

"Yes, like a slave."

"A slave?" Pedro said he had never heard of such a thing.

Rugg told him it was called trafficking, a business where girls were sometimes tricked, sometimes abducted, and then sold to men who used them as prostitutes.

"What miserable satyrs!" Pedro declared.

When Rugg asked if he knew of a red-light zone where women prostituted, Pedro said he had known one, having gone there as a young man and later, when his wife left him, but the brothel district had been shuttered for many years. "Now the women walk the streets and carry phones. Men take them to hourly motels or to cheap hotels like my brother's. The women are not slaves. They are whores who practice freely. I have not seen young girls among them."

Rugg said the sex trade was not a business as public as street prostitution, that it was in the shadows and harder to find. He said children were also abducted and killed for their organs, which were sold on the black market.

The old man's face went askew. "Organs?"

"For transplants."

"What unmothered shambles!" Pedro exclaimed. "What grub worm sons-of-disgraced-mothers!"

Rugg saw he had taken the old man into unfamiliar territory, a place where he would be of no assistance, a world too dark for his instincts. "First, the truck," Rugg said. "It is our best trail for now."

They got into the Ranger. The old man accelerated onto the highway. Rugg watched for a crossover in the median strip. Five kilometers passed. Ten, fifteen, twenty. Rugg checked the signposts, not finding the first return until the twenty-third kilometer — a dirt gap where the gavilleros could have crossed to the northbound lanes for retreat into Sonora. It seemed unlikely to Rugg that these men, after taking Rose, would travel such a distance to double-back. The likelihood large that they had continued south, perhaps across the state line.

"Your truck is a Ford, Mr. Rugg?"

Rugg described his pickup. He said it had a tow bar and extended mirrors — accessories that set it apart from others of its kind.

They drove. Rugg cast ahead for the first ranches. When he checked the side mirror, he saw the black-and-white Federal Police cruiser closing on them, the lightbar flashing. Rugg kept his eyes off the mirror, waiting for it to pass. Then the cruiser's squawk horn sounded, and he told Pedro to pull over.

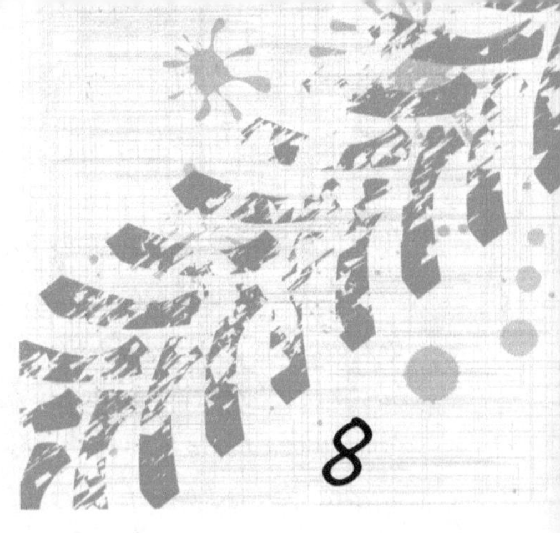

8

When I see the gringa, I'm in a girlie joint with Fer, XL, Nacho, and Perico. It's not a regular girlie joint where batos walk in off the street. It's a house turned into a girlie joint where you've got to be invited, and we're invited because XL knows the owner. In this joint the girls are young. No one asks if I'm old enough to be there, but the guy who takes our drink order asks me if I want Coke or Pepsi. Everyone laughs. I order a beer, bottled not canned, with salt and lime on the side. The house is dark and smoky. We sit in a big room where a trio plays in one corner. XL is the only one showing a pistol. Everyone else leaves his hardware in the ride after XL says he doesn't want any whores shot. El Sin doesn't come. Perico says El Sin never goes to girlie joints. When I spot her, she's sitting at another table with an old bato who is trying to put his arm around her. She pulls away, but he keeps reaching. She wears a fancy dress and shoes. Her hair is puffed up and her teeth don't *have the braces. She looks grown-up and skinnier since I saw her last. I drink the beer, and I wonder if she knows her badass gringo daddy is dead, and I wonder if she has a mother who cries for her. The old bato keeps trying to squeeze her and she keeps pushing him away. Then a square-headed pelado dressed in a suit gets up from the bar and goes to their table. His neck is sunk into his shoulders, which reminds me of a gorilla. He speaks to the gringa, and whatever he says makes her face go crooked. After he walks way, she lets the old bato reel her in.*

By then the whores have come to our table. XL asks for the youngest. A small girl steps forward. When he asks her age, she says thirteen. The other girls call her a liar. "She's twelve," one of them says. XL sits her on his knee. "You can ride there for now," he says. Then he asks the girls which one of them has worked in the joint the longest. They look at the tall girl in the group. XL points to me. "That's Rayo," he tells her. "Go to him. He has never gone boom." That gets a whoop from everyone. I feel my face get hot. "Not my first time," I protest, but the deal is done. The tall girl sits on my lap. XL tells me I can sit on hers if I want, which gets another laugh. The whore takes a sip from my beer. She smells like fruit — what kind, I'm not sure. Everyone takes a girl. XL orders more drinks. When I look at the table where the gringa sat, it's empty.

I don't ask the tall girl her name because I know she won't give me the real one. I've heard enough about whores from Perico to know they are like us in at least one way — they wear masks at their jobs.

The trio comes to our table. They play corridas and rancheras. I drink another beer. When the tall girl pulls me off the chair and leads me away, XL calls out, "Your premier is paid, Rayo." The well-dressed gorilla watches us leave. She takes me out a back door and across a patio. It's dark. I hear trickling water from somewhere. We go to a building that's lit like a motel, the doors in row, each with a number. "What's wrong with you?" she asks as she pulls me along, walking too fast for me to keep up. I tell her I have a bad foot. We stop in front of one of the doors. "So that's why they call you Speedy," she says.

The room is painted blue. It has a bed and a bathroom and the same fruity smell as the girl. She tells me to wait while she goes to the bathroom. On the wall there's a clock. I lay on the bed and take in the ceiling, where I see myself in a mirror. I feel the beer in my head. The clock ticks. When the tall girl comes out of the bathroom, she's wearing only a towel. She's not so tall without her shoes. She asks me why I'm still dressed, and I tell her she's not old enough to boss me around. She says she's sixteen. I say that means you're fourteen, like me, so nobody is bossing nobody. She sits on the bed and points to the wall clock. "You have until eight." I check my watch and tell her the clock is wrong. "Thirty minutes," she says before she takes off the towel and lays down beside me, which is all she needs to do for things to start fast and finish faster. The ceiling mirror makes it weird. Without getting into details, the experience chases the beer from my head. The tall girl goes to the bathroom. I dress and sit on the bed. When she comes back, her face is painted, and she has more fruit smell. "Time's up," she says.

In the salon Perico sits alone at our table. He's got XL's pistol and he's watching the room but mostly the front door. "How was the premier?" he jokes. If I know anything, I know that whatever I tell Perico gets retold, so I make sure he hears the truth a second time. "It's not my first!" I tell him. He grins and orders me a beer. I sip it, looking around the salon. The place is full. A highway cop sits with a girl. He doesn't wear his uniform, but I recognize him. He's a big cop. I've seen him on patrol near the state line. Sometimes he parks his cruiser at the tollbooths at Estación Don, but he never stops our crew. I don't see the gringa or the old bato. Being a granddaddy may get him more time in the room. The tall whore already sits with another customer. She doesn't look at me. While Perico and I wait for the rest of the crew to return, I spot a girl who looks familiar. I watch her, and when she looks back, I recognize her. She's a bata we lifted on a job outside of Guamúchil the month before. She's not a gringa, but an out-of-state girl we pulled from a ride with Jalisco plates. I remember her because she told El Sin to shoot her before they pushed her into the chase car. "Don't take me! Shoot me!" she screamed. But El Sin didn't shoot her, and here she is all calmed down and working in the same girlie joint as the gringa, who was also lifted by El Sin, which seems less like a coincidence and more like an arrangement.

I point to the square-headed pelado who stands by the bar. "Who's the gorilla in the suit?" I ask. Perico laughs. "Boss man," he says. "These are his girls." I finish the beer. When I check the salon again, I see the gringa return with the old bato. He pulls her by the hand to a table near the bar, where they sit. The old bato orders a drink. The gringa stares at nothing, like she's blind. Her face makes me think of her picture, the one I saw in the passport, where she looks like she hasn't lived a sad day in her life. Gone that girl.

RUGG TOLD THE OLD MAN to tell the highway cops that they were coming from Navojoa. "Do not speak of Rose." He remained in the Ranger while Pedro got down and walked to the police cruiser. Rugg recognized the black-and-white as the one seen at the tollplaza, the call number the same.

From his pocket he removed two five-hundred-peso bills, which he folded. The bundled cash from the telegraph office Rugg had wedged under the front seat between the frame and the cushion. When Pedro returned, he said the cops wanted to see the bill of sale. Rugg took the invoice from the glove box. He handed it to the old man with the folded bills. He said it would be better if the police didn't get out of the cruiser.

"I told them I forgot my license." Pedro explained. "But they want proof the truck isn't stolen."

"That is proof," Rugg said.

Pedro took the bill of sale to the cruiser. Rugg heard his thin voice, the winded narration interrupted by one of the cops. Rugg glanced at the console. In a cupholder lay the Remington casing lifted by the old man from the

roadside. Rugg put it in his pocket with the others he had saved.

The big officer who approached the passenger side wished him a good afternoon.

"Buenas tardes," Rugg responded.

He asked Rugg to step down from the truck for a routine verification. Rugg descended and retook the crutches. When the officer saw Rugg's leg, he apologized for the inconvenience.

"No problem," Rugg replied. He observed Pedro standing beside the second cop at the cruiser. The cop wrote on a block tablet laid on the hood. Pedro spoke and spoke. The cop nodded as he wrote. Rugg gazed at the desert. The sun low. A traffic ticket the best of all outcomes, he thought.

The big officer opened the driver's door and knelt to inspect the metal identification plate affixed to the jamb. He held the bill of sale in one hand. Rugg leaned on his crutches and took in the highway. The cash not in plain view. The invoice bona fide. He had verified the chassis and the motor numbers at the time of the purchase. The officer left the cab to raise the truck hood. He lifted a flashlight from his belt and beamed the engine compartment. When he found the motor block's serial number, he compared it to the one written on the bill of sale. After he closed the hood, he came to where Rugg stood. He did not hand over the bill of sale. "Thank you for your cooperation," he said.

"No problem," repeated Rugg.

The big officer not as big as Rugg without the crutches. His face road wise and past praying for. No name printed on his uniform. Rugg guessed he was the senior cop.

"You friend's truck has no plates," he said. "We are checking for stolen vehicles."

Rugg said nothing. He knew about trucks with no plates. He knew stolen.

The officer pointed to Rugg's leg. "What happened?"

"An accident," Rugg answered.

A nod from the big cop. "Qué lástima."

Rugg silent. Not for him to weigh in on pity.

"Your friend says you are coming from Navojoa," said the officer.

"Correct," Rugg replied.

The officer returned the flashlight to his belt. "You are American? Or Canadian?"

Rugg met his gaze. "American."

The big cop smiled. "Have you been in Mexico long?"

"A few weeks," Rugg replied.

The officer complimented Rugg on his Spanish. His gaze lingered on Rugg's cap. "May I have your name?"

Rugg considered it likely Pedro had not given them the money. "Bob Rugg."

The big cop looked plainly at him. "Are you a tourist, Mr. Rugg?"

Rugg said he was.

"You look familiar. Have I stopped you before?"

Rugg's face gave away nothing. He knew the cop hadn't seen him at the tollplaza. "Maybe another trip," he said. "I have come before."

The officer smiled. "Maybe. I don't remember the face of every stop, but yours, I think, I have seen somewhere."

When Rugg said all gringos looked alike, the officer laughed. "True," he agreed. "Except the ones on crutches."

They waited for the other cop to finish writing the ticket. The old man talked lustily about his bus driving days on the Tijuana route.

"Your friend is shameless," the big officer remarked. "He drives on a federal highway without plates or license, and then he offers us money to look away. In your country, that is a serious crime, yes? To bribe a police officer. A man goes to jail for that, does he not?"

Rugg said it was likely, unless there was entrapment.

"Yes, a trap. But the police are careful, right?"

"They fear prison," Rugg said. "It makes them careful."

The big cop nodded. "Of course. Very interesting. Are you a lawyer, Mr. Rugg?"

Rugg shook his head.

"A policeman, maybe?"

"No, a pilot. Retired."

"A pilot? That is a good job. Pilots make much money. I hope you did not fly drugs." He grinned, eyeing Rugg. "I am joking, of course. We have such pilots here, but they do not live long. Piloting is dangerous work, I hear."

Rugg shrugged as best he could. "It depends on the pilot," he said. He shifted on his crutches, feeling his leg large, the dressing damp. Soon the boot sock would stain. Then the pantleg. The big officer stood with gravity on his side.

"Was your accident in a plane, Mr. Rugg?"

"Car," Rugg corrected.

A thread, he thought. How he hung here. He knew the big officer had seized on the peculiarity of a one-footed gringo riding with an old man in a truck purchased that day. Rugg glanced at the pistol snugged in a duty holster on the officer's hip, the holster with its thumb-break unsecured. The big cop cocky or just careless around a man on crutches. Rugg certain he would have to shoot both cops should they try to detain him. The old man his witness, and then what?

He loosely gripped the crutch handles. At the cruiser Pedro signed the paperwork. The ticketing cop a boy-faced patrolman who Rugg reckoned was faster with a pen than a gun. A cop likely overmatched by ambush.

"Mr. Rugg, may I trouble you for some identification?" asked the big officer. "Your driver's license. Or your pilot's license. They are different, right?"

Rugg said he had left his wallet at the hotel.

"OK. Do you carry your passport and visa?"

"At the hotel," Rugg answered.

The big officer lamented the inconvenience of such an oversight. "You said you have visited Mexico before?"

"Yes."

"Then you know a tourist must carry these documents at all times. Is it not the same for a foreigner in your country? If I am stopped by your police, will I be asked for my papers? I think so. And if I do not have them, it is complicated, yes? The immigration authorities are notified. I am detained, maybe deported. There is no end of trouble and time lost. Do you agree?"

"Of course," Rugg replied. "It was careless. I will be sure to carry them."

The old man and the ticketing cop stood beside them. Rugg saw the cop's weapon with the retaining strap fastened. The revolver a .38. The big officer held to the bill of sale. He smiled. "I believe you," he said. "We forget things. Your friend forgot his license. These problems can be remedied."

Rugg nodded. *Finally.*

"What hotel are you staying at, Mr. Rugg?"

When Rugg said he did not recall the name, the officer looked amused. "You do not know where you are staying?"

"I arrived late. It has no sign."

"Hotel San Carlos," the old man interjected. "I took down the sign for business reasons."

The big officer instructed his partner to put the old man in the back of the cruiser. The partner pointed Pedro away from the Ranger.

"For what?" protested the old man.

"For shameless," the big officer replied. "And for talking too much." He turned to Rugg. "Are you carrying a firearm, Mr. Rugg?"

Rugg's face with measured surprise. "No," he said, voice neutral. He observed the old man seated in the cruiser. The ticketing cop stood by the door.

"Is there a firearm in the vehicle?"

"No."

The big cop nodded. "I'm sure you know we have strict firearm laws in Mexico."

Rugg said he knew.

"Good. We have recent reports of assaults and carjackings on this stretch. You do not look like a carjacker, Mr. Rugg, but our job is to keep the highway safe. To that end, we are conducting vehicular searches on all road stops. It will take but a moment. I apologize for the inconvenience."

The sun set. The highway without witness. Rugg knew the search would reveal the bundled money under the seat. The spent casings on him.

"I must ask you to empty your pockets. It is protocol."

"Of course."

The big cop pointed to Rugg's leg. "Are you injured, Mr. Rugg? You have blood on your pants."

Rugg shook his head. He didn't look down. "It bleeds sometimes."

"From your accident?"

"From a dog bite," Rugg replied.

"Ah."

He crutched closer to the officer, within reach of his holstered weapon. "How much?" he asked in a low voice.

"Excuse me?" the officer replied.

Rugg calculated that a blow struck with the crutches under the cop's jaw would send both hands off his hips. He eyed the duty holster but was unable to spot the safety. "How much do you want?" he asked.

The officer's face a mask. "Are you offering me a bribe, Mr. Rugg?"

Rugg paired the crutches under one arm. "Yes."

"That could be trouble for you."

"Both of us are being careful," Rugg said.

"I am always careful."

"I see that. What's your price?"

"My price?"

"To let us retake the road."

The officer glanced toward the cruiser. "Twenty thousand pesos."

Not a calculation, Rugg decided, rather a number grabbed from the sky and meant to flatten him. He shook his head. "That is not possible."

He grinned. "Anything is possible, Mr. Rugg. We are in Mexico. It is possible that I arrest you and your shameless friend. It is possible I find a weapon in the vehicle, or drugs, or dirty money, or all three. It is possible you resist arrest and I shoot you both."

Rugg replied that many outcomes were possible, but not all were known. "I want one favorable for both of us," he added.

The officer retreated a step. "Twenty is favorable. My partner and I share. We also take dollars, if that's more convenient."

Rugg shook his head. "I don't have that much."

"Are you pretending to be a poor gringo, Mr. Rugg?"

"I am a poor gringo pretending to be a nice one," Rugg said.

The officer laughed. "I think you are a gringo negotiating like a Mexican."

"Six," Rugg offered.

The officer called it an insult.

At the cruiser the junior cop and Pedro conversed. Rugg calculated the shooting distance. He said, "You will leave us without cash for gas and tolls."

"Mr. Rugg, do I look like a fool? You are riding in a truck sold today to an old man who wears huaraches and has no license. I think he is the driver of the gringo who bought the truck, and I think if I search the gringo and his truck I will find the money he claims not to have." The officer extracted from his pocket a handful of coins. "I will pay your toll if that worries you."

The bills Rugg took from his pocket still wound in a rubber band. "This is ten," he said. "Search the truck if you want. It's all my cash." He hopped a step closer, holding the money for the cop to take with his shooting hand. Behind him rose the sound of an approaching vehicle.

The officer smiled. "What if I take it and still search you, Mr. Rugg?"

Rugg said that would be complicated for both parties.

"Do you think? How so?"

"Because I will tell your mother you are a dirty cop who does not keep his word."

He watched the smile drop from the officer's face.

"What do you mean? My mother is dead."

"Then you will tell her yourself," Rugg replied.

The vehicle sped past. Rugg shifted the crutches. He had not planned it so, but nothing in the past weeks had gone as planned. What could be lost here not greater than losing Rose for good. Then the big cop nodded. "OK," he agreed. "Ten."

Rugg said nothing. He held to the money.

"My word is good," the cop said. "I will not disappoint my mother today."

Rugg said today was all that mattered.

The big cop told Rugg that he should get into the truck to finish their business.

He ascended and cracked the vent window, wedging the folded bills into the opening. The cop took the money and put it in his pocket without counting it before he gestured to his partner to send the old man. He handed Rugg the bill of sale. "You are a lucky gringo, Mr. Rugg."

Rugg said their luck was shared.

At the driver's door Pedro shook hands with the junior partner. Rugg didn't offer his hand to the big cop. He said, "You know my name and where to find me, Officer, but I do not know yours or where to find you."

"Why would you need to find me, Mr. Rugg?"

"In case I need your help."

"Help?"

"Yes. Help finding something I've lost."

"And what is that?"

"I will let you know if I don't find it."

The big cop smiled. "Mr. Rugg, it is better for you not to cross my path again. If I had wanted to know your business, I would have made it my business. What I know is that you are a gringo with one foot and no papers. You should leave Mexico — today, tomorrow — before something bad happens to you. If I am the dog that bites, you are the one that bleeds. On this road there are bigger dogs than me, dogs that smell blood."

Rugg said he would take it into consideration. Then he told Pedro to retake the road.

The old man waited for the cruiser to pass them before he spoke. "Two five-hundreds don't get you far with these federal fellows," he said.

Rugg looked at him. "You gave them the money?"

"I did. The big one took it and gave half to the young one. 'For dinner,' he said. No shame in that big one. The other is a cub."

They drove.

"Maybe it was a bad idea to give them the hotel," Pedro remarked.

Rugg said that bad ideas did not always bear bad results. He said the cops had gotten a good look at the Ranger. "They will find us if they want."

"If you desire to change hotels, Mr. Rugg, that is OK."

"It is a good hotel, Pedro. Almost perfect."

They headed south, night fallen when they left the highway and drove into the first town. They stopped at a corner grocery, where they bought bottled water and bagged chips. Rugg took the antibiotic before he directed Pedro to commence a crisscross route from one dirt street to the next until the back of the town was reached.

"A white Ford, four-door, with big mirrors," he said, reminding the old man. Then they looked for Rugg's truck.

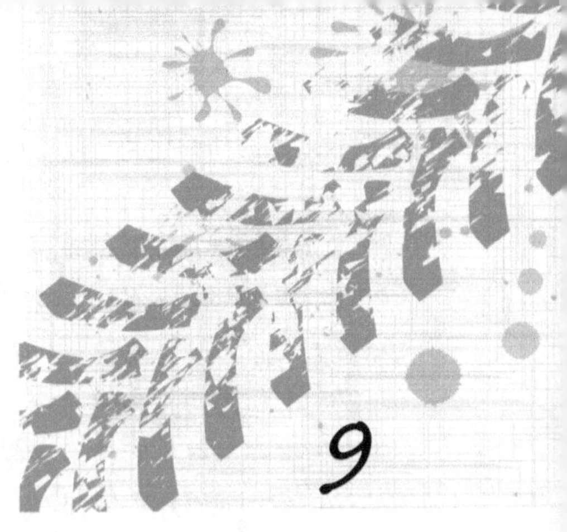

9

Güero del Café says good girls like bad guys because they want to meet God. I'm not sure what he means, unless meeting God means dying, which he delivers regularly. I don't know anything about God, but I do know something about Güero del Café — he's crazy. His eyes give it away. They're too black for such a white face. He is El Sin's right-hand devil, and the guy who takes care of the dirty business, from shooting to cutting. He carries a knife on his belt and takes trophies to show he's done a job — the tongue from a snitch, the hand from a thief, an eye from a bato who sees something he shouldn't. Sometimes he sends messages to rival crews. He'll hang a toy car on the neck of a carjacker or leave a cigarette in a bato's mouth to show he got a last smoke. I've never seen his devilry, but I've heard of it. Güero del Café likes his drugs, which El Sin lets him keep for the hell he visits on batos. The drugs rot his teeth and make him grin all the time. He thinks he can speak English, which he can't, but he spits out what he knows all the same. His words sound the way a dog would speak English, if a dog could talk. He's the one who killed the badass gringo and took the toes for trophies — this, according to Perico, who keeps his ear to the ground, like the Indian scouts in the Old West movies.

It's Perico who tells us that we're going to Guasave to work the highway to Sinaloa de Leyva and the roads to Ocoroni and San Blas. We set up moving checkpoints where we pretend to be state judicial cops in charge of enforcing the public safety and checking for stolen vehicles and illegal firearms. Perico calls us coyotes watching the coop. He grew up on a ranch, so he knows about animals and how to kill chickens. Our crew runs in three rides, and we carry police beacons that stick to the cab roofs. We sleep in the day and work in the late night, when the only batos on the roads are the ones who shouldn't be or the ones who have the bad luck to be. As a rule, family batos don't travel at those hours. Our roadblocks look like the ones cops put up with warning cones and signboards that say Puesto de Control and Retén Judicial. We set up at speed bumps and railroad crossings and any straight stretch between two curves. XL and the lieutenants carry cop shields on their belts. The real cops know where we work, and they keep clear of us for the most part. If they show up, XL tells them to get lost. We stop every ride on the road — late model, junk model, and models in between. Our front man makes the drivers and the passengers get down, and then he frisks them. XL checks the papers and identifications before he interrogates each bato, asking where he comes from, where he goes to, where he lives, what's his day job, what's his business on the road. Sometimes he takes a bato off by himself and talks to him. Sometimes he gets on his phone while the bato waits. Our crew searches the ride for weapons, checking under the seats and behind the door panels and in the motor compartment.

My job is to crawl beneath the ride with a flashlight and to look where the underside has been cooked to hide something. Shiny bolts on an old gas tank are a giveaway. A muddy driveshaft with clean U-joints is another. It's a dirty job, but I'm the skinniest and youngest. Güero del Café says I make a good roach because I can't walk straight, which is the kind of craziness he speaks. He doesn't call me Rayo like everyone else. He calls me Chueco — which means Crooked. When he sees my pistol, he asks if I know how to shoot it. I tell him I've shot it plenty. His rotten-toothed grin opens into a laugh. "But have you cut one down? Have you got one on your face?" he asks. I don't answer. He pulls the knife from his belt and shows it to me. It's a regular knife, except bigger. He wants me to hold it, but I don't. "Cuta bootifo de man ey," he says, which is dog-speaking nonsense to me. He knows I worked for Macho Prieto. He says MP was a blind fool and a good-for-nothing coward who finished like a whimpering woman. I don't like to hear it. It makes me think he's the one who left MP with parts missing in the cane field, doing it on El Sin's orders. I stay clear of his craziness as much as I can, which isn't easy.

Our crew works the Guasave checkpoints for a week, stopping all flavors of batos on the roads. No trouble finds us, and we don't find any, and no one tells me what trouble we're trying to find. Then one night outside Estación Naranjo, we stop two batos in a late-model Ford Lobo. The truck has no papers or plates. The two batos carry machine pistols and radios and they don't give XL a good reason for carrying them. He has them thrown into the bed of a pickup and he drives off with them, taking along his lieutenants and the grinning Güero del Café. The rest of our crew stays at the checkpoint. When XL returns, only one bato is in the pickup. The bato is barely able to stand after they drag him out of the truck bed. The lieutenants push and kick him back into the Lobo. One of his hands is wrapped with duct tape where his fingers are gone, but he still has his thumb. Güero del

Café shows off his new trophies. I'm not afraid to look at them — they're just fingers.

The cut bato drives off one-handed. We keep the machine pistols and radios. XL orders us to lift the roadblock, and we return to Los Mochis. Later Perico tells me that the trouble we were looking for goes by the name of Cali. Cali is a car thief who runs his own crew that boosts rides on turf that belongs to El Sin, which is an invasion El Sin won't overlook, and why he sent XL to check the roads for him. Instead of finding him, we found two of his batos. One got a message to take back to the celebrated Cali. The bato who didn't come back was a message too.

*T*WO DAYS THEY searched for Rugg's truck in the highway towns of the Sonoran borderland before they headed south into the Carrizo Valley, where they crisscrossed the dirt streets of ranches named for populist heroes and revolutionary apothegms. They stopped at taco stands and one-pump Pemex stations to feed and fuel, their hat brims pulled down, the old man told to curb his volubility. They saw many white Ford pickups, Rugg's four-door not among them. They slept in the Ranger, Rugg retreating to the truck bed where he lay and stared into overcast skies. He slept fitfully or not at all. In the mornings he redressed his leg, the bleeding diminished, the pain without end. The pocketed casings he threw out of the truck, their cold brass incrimination left to the acquittal of strangers, the calibers carried in his head. In every town he dialed her cell phone, to no response. He took in the street gatherings of idle men and boys, eyeing their slacked postures, the tilted sombreros, the reversed ball caps. He looked for one man who stood taller than the rest, his silver hair catching the light. He looked for a boy shoed in flashy sneakers who walked with a limp.

No suspect surfaced from among the idlers.

They drove the backroads, coming upon rustic fincas without apparent tenants, ideal for hideouts. Rugg got down to check for tire tracks, finding none that matched the tread pattern and the wheelbase of his Ford. Beyond the towns, the land a sketchwork of farms and campos, some with grain silos and tractor sheds but none with dwellings or farmhouses of the kind Rugg knew as a boy. When he asked the old man if the farmers lived on the land they cultivated, he said men with families did not reside on their farms for fear of being assaulted or kidnapped at night in solitary dwellings beyond the protection of the law. He said farmers preferred to live in the towns, where a false sense of security abided among the multitudes, and in proximity to the good-for-nothing police. Rugg told Pedro that he was too smart to be driving a bus or managing a hotel, that he should enter politics because he understood the fear and falsehood in men. The old man said he was smart enough to know he was a fool, like all men. Rugg nodded. "That makes you a sage, Pedro."

On the third evening, a Sunday, they visited the valley's only brothel in the ranch town of Chihuahuita. Before descending from the Ranger, the old man suggested he enter first to reconnoiter and prepare for any unpleasant surprises. Rugg shook his head. "You do not know my daughter." He crutched inside the low-roofed structure, stopping at the bar, where he turned to view the interior. A mound of sawdust lay in one corner, men standing before it to urinate. Curtained booths served for private rooms. Rugg sick to his stomach at the thought of finding her here. When he spotted no likeness, he told the old man to bring the manager. While he waited, the whore who approached him touched his good leg and asked him to buy her a drink. Rugg ordered a brandy and Coke. He said he sought the youngest girl in the lounge. She answered, "How young do you want?" Rugg said thirteen, preferably blonde. The whore grinned. "I can paint myself blonde and pretend to be thirteen," she offered. Rugg said he would get back to her the day she had a daughter old enough to work here. She swore at him before she left, taking her drink. When the manager came, Rugg asked if he had any gringas in his establishment. The manager said, "If gringas rained from the sky, none would fall here." He added that he welcomed new business opportunities, if Rugg proposed one. Rugg gave the manager his mobile number. He said he would pay for any gringa girl that fell from the sky or arrived otherwise in his employ. The manager agreed to call.

The next morning their return to the highway was delayed by a funeral procession, the mourners on foot and riding on horseback. Though the cortege occupied but half the road, the old man refused to pass, claiming it was bad luck to overtake the dead on their final journey, and so they followed the procession to the cemetery turnoff at the edge of town. Rugg took in the grief-wrenched and stoic faces. He heard the torn wails of women. The deceased a child, the casket a cloth-covered box upholstered in pink.

By midday they traversed the last of the valley ranches and the highway towns of San Miguel and Nuevo San Miguel. Rugg directed the old man to return to the city. At the hotel Carlos reported new phone calls from Rugg's sister and Eric White. When Rugg asked if anyone had visited the hotel looking for him, Carlos shook his head.

"Please let me know if anyone does," Rugg said.

He ascended to his room, where he showered. Road dust and dried blood to show for his search. He sat on the chair to cut the leg stitches with the nail scissors, removing them with the forceps. The skin flaps knitted, the transtibial cut roughly seamed. He disinfected and bandaged the wound before he cut the spandex tops off two clean boot socks and pulled them over the stump. He dressed in new jeans and recounted the wired money, breaking out cash to pocket, using the dressing tape to affix the unopened bundles to the inside of the bedframe. He checked the window for locks, finding the sash nailed to the frame. He surveyed the street. Downstairs he found the old man asleep in the lobby chair, no change in his attire.

They drove to the Telmex building, where Rugg paid for thirty minutes of internet access at a kiosk terminal with a fixed trackball and an imbedded keyboard. His inbox with mail from Sue, her clipped recriminations: *Why can't you call? Where's Rose?* Rugg replied: *All well. Returning soon.* She had sent the scans of his pilot's license, Rose's school ID, and their birth certificates. His hard face stared back at him from the license taken in the days when he commanded the sky and all the odds against him. How he glared at fate. Nothing horizoned then that could bring him down. He gazed at Rose's sixth-grade school picture. Braids and braces. Those wild eyes. So much of her mother yet to come.

The clerk at the Telmex kiosk printed the birth certificates and made color copies of the license and the library card. Rugg asked him to enlarge Rose's picture and to print it separately on photo paper. With borrowed scissors he cut out the front and back sides of the photocopied license. He aligned them back to back, trimming the edges to the actual size before he instructed the clerk to laminate the copy in the thickest butterfly pouch. The laminated replica warm when the clerk handed it to him. Rugg put it in his wallet.

In the truck he showed Rose's picture to Pedro.

"A beautiful girl," he said.

Rugg nodded.

"She does not look like you."

"No, like her mother."

He put the copies of her photo inside a purchased folder and he directed the old man to drive to the Red Cross clinic. At the clinic's reception desk Rugg presented Rose's photo to the woman on duty. He explained that the girl was his daughter, who had been involved in a highway accident near the state line. He gave the date and time of the accident and he asked if the records for ambulance calls made on that day could be shown to him. The receptionist said all calls for highway accidents came from the 066 emergency services, a department of the State Police. She referred Rugg to the police dispatcher for call logs. She studied the photo, not recognizing Rose, but she offered to show it to the drivers and the paramedics working in the clinic. Some came to the reception desk to see the photo. Young medics in white uniforms, eager to aid. None recognized Rose. When Rugg asked if they recognized him, the medics assessed him, his crutched presence. All but one shook their heads. A youth with two volunteer patches on his uniform said, "Are you the Canadian from the boat accident in Topolobampo?" Rugg said he had lost his leg on the highway near the Sonoran border. The medic apologized, saying he had not gone to any highway pickups. One of the group asked what had happened to the girl. Rugg said she had left the highway after the accident, that he was checking the clinics on the chance she might have been injured. When they asked if he had visited the Hospital Civil, he nodded. He wrote his mobile number on the photo, leaving it with the receptionist and requesting as a great favor that it be shown in turn to the off-duty staff. "Please call if they recognize her," he said.

Outside, Pedro asked if they were going to the police.

"Not yet," Rugg answered. When he inquired if the Hospital Civil was the only hospital in the city, Pedro said there was a pricey private facility where the doctors charged to look at the walls. On the drive Rugg thought about how far his world had contracted that another foreigner — his foot lost in a boating accident — had come to be confused with him.

At the private hospital the staff knew nothing of Rose. He left another photo with his number. No long shot too long, Rugg decided.

They spent the remaining daylight hours visiting the used car lots. Rugg left the old man to waylay and engage the salesmen while he crutched between the rowed cars, looking for his Ford — with or without extended mirrors, perhaps repainted. He knew that stolen vehicles were most often exhibited at the back of a lot, where they were sold to less-discerning customers and to those who knew they were stolen.

His truck not spotted in any lot.

When Pedro asked what Rugg would do if the truck was not found, Rugg said he would track down the perpetrators without the truck, if it came to that.

The old man nodded. "Maybe the truck has left the state."

"Maybe."

"Maybe Rose too. I'm sorry to be the one to say so."

Rugg said he had considered the possibility.

"Without the truck, Mr. Rugg, we will need help. These whoremothers hide in plain day. They eat on the street. We might sit beside them and not know who they are. A tip may be the only way to find them."

Rugg agreed that a tip would help.

At dusk he asked Pedro to drive him to the city airport, where he descended and stood at the security fence. He saw private aircraft parked on the apron. Single-engine props. A student trainer. The tarmac sentineled by soldiers and a combat vehicle. Inside the terminal they stood before the destination board. Travelers observed them — a sandaled old man, a one-footed gringo — an odd pair of pilgrims come to contemplate airborne wonders. Rugg checked the boards for commercial flights to Hermosillo, finding a daily departure on a national carrier. He noted the flight number and departure time. Back in the truck, they drove to a hardware store, where the old man got down to purchase for Rugg a roll of reinforced duct tape.

10

I'm on a crew with El Sin when I get my first shots at a bato. He wears a white sombrero and a yellow shirt, and he drives a metallic gold Hilux. This bato gets noticed. When he sees me limp into the street, he makes the choice to stop instead of running me down. Running me down might have saved him, but he decides to share the road and yield to a crippled kid. He recognizes the mistake as soon as he brakes. His eyes jump from me to the cutoff car, where El Sin rides shotgun. I watch the bato through the windshield. His mustache is gray. The look on his face is one I've seen on other batos caught by surprise. A sick look. Dogs get it when they're jumped. Our chase car bumpers the back of the Hilux, so the bato can't reverse. I see El Sin descend loose and easy and not in a hurry, no mask on his face. He holds a pistol at his side. None of our crew follow because those are his orders. He moves to the driver's window, which is down, and he tells the bato to get out.

El Sin doesn't shout. His voice is flat, like he's telling time off his watch. The bato obeys. He doesn't raise his hands over his head the way some do. El Sin lifts the pistol and shoots him low. The bato grabs his stomach and drops to his knees before he doubles over. His sombrero falls to the asphalt. Blood leaks around his hands and turns his yellow shirt into a bad sunset. El Sin kicks him onto his back. When the bato raises his hands to cover his face, El Sin shoots him low again and puts his boot on the bato's chest. He leans over and speaks to him in a whisper, and then he stands straight before he shoots him in the face. I'm slow to get back to our ride, watching the bato die.

When El Sin turns, he sees me. His face has nothing on it. He's a scary, no-face Sin. With his pistol he motions for me to come. Traffic backs up. The panicky run. The ordinary duck. "Shoot him," El Sin tells me when I come. My Colt is tucked under my shirt. I pull it, flip the safety, and point. I see his jaw blown sideways where El Sin shot him. The gray mustache is torn in half. His eyes are open, but he doesn't move or gurgle. The cracks in the street fill with his blood. I fire three rounds at his chest. The two that hit him make the bato twitch. The one that misses hits under his armpit. The shot spits asphalt into the air. Some hits El Sin, but he doesn't flinch. "Again," he says, not looking at me. I empty the Colt into the bato, including two in his pants. My hand doesn't jitter. When El Sin heads back to our ride, he's in no hurry. I follow, thinking I just shot a dead bato but not very well. I'm not sure why El Sin made me jump in, unless it's for the practice. He scuffs his boot on the pavement before he climbs into our ride. Inside, he says, "Let's eat." We leave the Hilux in the street with the driver's door open. I never find out the name of the bato or why El Sin ultimated him. Later it's not the bato's face I remember or how his gray mustache split in two. It's the boot print left on his shirtfront that I remember, the one El Sin put there when he stepped on him. A bloody print.

THEY DROVE TO THE pawn shops nearest the Red Cross clinic and the Hospital Civil. The old man remained in the Ranger while Rugg got down. At each shop he asked to see the watches. Two blocks from the hospital, he found his Breitling in La Casa de Empeño Fácil, a shop with barred windows and a roll-down steel curtain on the door. Rugg examined the watch before he slipped it on his wrist. The broker complimented him on his good taste. Rugg handed it back, and then he asked to see the wedding bands. The bands displayed in bulk on a foam jewelry tray. Rugg took each ring from the tray and checked for engravings inside the shank. When he found his band, he asked the broker for its price and for the price of the watch. He did not try on the ring. The broker brought a loupe to read the carat weight before he quoted a price for both. Rugg asked if he was the proprietor.

"At your service," he replied.

No other customers arrived at the shop. Rugg leaned across the counter and spoke. "I will buy both if you tell me where you got them."

The broker smiled. "They come from people who need money more than they need the things you see here," he said.

"Do you know if they are stolen?" Rugg asked.

"I do not sell stolen merchandise, sir."

Rugg nodded. He said the watch and the ring had been stolen from him four weeks earlier.

"You are mistaken," the broker replied.

"No mistake," Rugg said. "The watch's bezel is dented from a high-altitude fall. The inscription on the ring is Latin. *Tamquam alter idem.* It is from Cicero."

The broker said he had no idea what Rugg was talking about. "Can you prove they were yours?"

"I just did."

"They are not stolen. You will not get a better price by saying so."

Rugg said he was not negotiating the price. "It is information I want. Can you tell me who brought them here?"

"They were not pawned. They were sold. I do not ask names."

"Can you tell me if it was a man or a woman? A boy?"

The dealer said he could not recall.

Rugg turned from the counter. "You may keep them," he said. Then he crutched to the door.

"Un momento," the broker replied.

Rugg stopped. Through the door glass he saw the old man standing by the truck.

"I don't know about the ring," the broker said. "We buy many rings. The watch I remember. It was brought by a woman. She said it belonged to her father who died."

Rugg stood by the door. "Did the woman work at the Hospital Civil?"

He shrugged. "We get business from the hospital. I won't deny it. Families must settle a patient's bill. There are nurses who receive gifts from grateful patients."

"Right." Rugg returned to the counter. He took cash from his pocket and dealt the sum. The broker counted the money before he handed over the items. Rugg slid the ring on his finger and looked at it. He pocketed the Timex and put on the watch. "Do you sell firearms?" he asked. Rugg had observed the bulge of a handgun under the man's untucked shirtfront. The weapon likely holstered.

The broker smiled again. "That question," he said, "begs another. Are you Mexican?"

"I am," Rugg replied.

"Then, yes, I sell firearms. Only to Mexicans."

Rugg said in that case he would buy the handgun the man carried poorly concealed under his shirt.

The smile fell from the broker's face. "It is not for sale."

"I will give you ten thousand pesos if it is not a revolver, ammunition included. You may keep the holster."

The broker stared at Rugg. "I think you are a gringo pretending to be a Mexican who needs a gun."

"I think you are a fence pretending to be pawnbroker. We both are who we say we aren't."

The broker considered this before he spoke. "If I sell you a gun, you could shoot me and take back your money."

Rugg said if he had wanted to shoot him, he would have secured the gun as soon as he identified his watch. He told the broker that to avoid a double-cross, he should unload the weapon he carried, and he should retrieve the second gun he kept behind the counter.

"How do you know I have a second gun?"

"I guessed."

"What of the police? It is illegal for me to sell a firearm. I could go to jail."

"I think you are out of jail because of the police, which is why you sell stolen watches and contraband weapons."

"So you know my business, do you?"

Rugg said he knew only what he saw. "Do we have a deal? Or do I go elsewhere?"

The broker walked to the door and locked it. When he returned, he reached beneath his shirtfront and pulled out the weapon. He released the magazine and set the pistol before Rugg. From under the counter he pulled the second weapon and holstered it. He took a box of cartridges from a file cabinet and put it in a paper bag.

The gun was a Smith & Wesson Shield with an extended-capacity magazine for a full grip and the upgraded I-Dot sights for low light. Rugg did not pick it up. He knew the pistol was a good conceal carry that required no holster. He asked the broker if he had the flush magazine that came with the model.

"I have only what you see," he replied.

When Rugg asked to inspect the rounds, the broker handed him the paper bag. The cartridge box almost full, the loads standard American Eagle 9mm Lugar. Better for plinking than killing.

"I will pay extra for hollow points," Rugg said.

"I have only what you see."

Rugg closed the bag and took the money from his pocket a second time. The broker collected the cash and counted it again before he put it in a drawer.

"I think you are a gringo looking for trouble."

"Mexicano," Rugg corrected.

"Ah, sí. Mexicano."

After the broker placed the pistol in the paper bag with the cartridges, he carried it to the door, which he unlocked. "Good hunting," he said.

Rugg took the bag and left the shop, hearing the roll-down steel door drop behind him.

The old man sat in the truck. "Now, there's a house full of trinkets," he observed, "and a rat running it."

Rugg set the bag on the truck floor. He showed Pedro the watch and ring.

"Yours?"

He nodded.

"That's good news. Did he say where he got them?"

"He did. It was brought by a woman."

"A woman?"

Rugg said she may have worked in the hospital where he had been laid up.

Pedro shook his head. "I've heard the hospitals are full of vultures. They know the dead don't check the hour."

A month since Rugg had worn the wedding band, the ring large on his finger. He played with it as the old man drove to the hotel.

"I guess that leaves us no closer to the dirty sons-of-fornication," Pedro said.

Rugg did not tell the old man that his search of pawn shops had been aimed at finding a weapon as much as a lead.

"No closer," he agreed. He said that one of the gavilleros — a masked boy not much older than his daughter — had taken his wallet but had left him the watch and the ring.

"A boy?"

"A boy with a limp who wore a silver-plated pistol."

"There's a lead," Pedro said.

"Maybe."

They drove. The old man did not ask about the paper bag. At the hotel Rugg directed him to park the Ranger behind the building. In the lobby Pedrito manned the desk. He reported that a man had come to the hotel to ask if a gringo was registered. "I told him the señor was no longer a guest."

"Was he a cop?" the old man asked.

The son shrugged. "He didn't say."

"What did he look like?"

Young Pedro described a big man. "He acted like a boss."

The old man looked at Rugg. "What do you think?"

Rugg said, "I think Pedrito did well."

In his room he laid the folder with her photos on the chair. He checked the bedframe, finding the cash bundles where he had taped them. Rugg loaded the gun and tested the sights with the lights off. He practiced a clean draw off one crutch. Then without crutches. With lengths of dressing tape he fashioned a rudimentary stripper clip to carry the unboxed rounds on his good leg.

Downstairs he told the old man that he was going out for several hours, that he preferred to leave the Ranger parked. He asked young Pedro to call a taxi.

11

I ask Perico when he's going back to the girlie joint run by the gorilla in the suit. He laughs and calls me a speedy rooster. He says there are lots of girlie joints to visit, that he will take me to others but not to the same one twice, because frequenting the same hole gets noticed by cops and competitors, which is bad for business. He says what I need is an older, more experienced woman to steer my train, not some underage chica who misses her bicycle. When I tell him that I like the joint we visited because the girls are pretty and friendly, Perico laughs again. "Pretty is paint and friendly is the job," he jokes. He says a whore is done whoring if she doesn't smile. I shut up about the girlie joint because I don't want to sound choosy. What he says about whores being friendly makes me think the gringa won't last on the job. Not with her sad face. Not that it matters.

UGG TOLD THE TAXISTA to take him to where there were girls. He rode with the gun tucked under his shirt. On his head the cap pulled down.

The taxista regarded him in the rearview "Dancing girls?"

"Bad girls," Rugg said. He said he would pay curb time if the fare was reasonable. When the taxista asked for the estimated wait, Rugg answered that he wished to visit as many clubs as were open at this hour, however long that took.

They agreed on an advance and an hourly rate. The taxista said, "You're not from around here, are you?"

"I am becoming from around here," Rugg replied.

At the first club, his entrance provided a momentary diversion from the floor show — a crutched man afoot to syncopated rhythms. Rugg took a corner table distant from the elevated platform where four women performed body climbs on two chromed poles. Rugg ordered a drink. When the waiter brought it, he paid, declining to open a tab. He asked if there were any gringas who danced in the club.

"No, but we have blondes who look like gringas," the waiter replied. "Should I send one?"

Rugg shook his head. He drank, taking in the tables and booths. No girl approached his corner. On the platform the dancers took tips from the men who jostled to touch their glistening nakedness. Rugg observed the girls who departed with customers and those who returned alone, their faces the same, none young enough to be new to the business. He took out his mobile and dialed her number, and then he studied his drink, remembering how Rose loved to dance. She danced at school. She danced in her room. She danced with her mother, both barefooted on the carpet, their laughter without measure. Not once had he danced with Rose.

He left without finishing the drink. On the street he spat the whiskey taste from this mouth. Back in the taxi he rode with his gaze beyond the window on the women who trolled the sidewalks in shimmering dresses and peaked shoes, their painted faces turned to him with beckoning ennui. Rugg saw each only for who she was not.

They crisscrossed the city from club to club, no dive overlooked. His leg throbbed. The gun rode cold under his shirt. In each girlie joint he ordered a drink and asked for gringas. He dialed her number. A search without success.

In the taxi the driver asked Rugg if he was looking for something special. His query voiced with guarded concern.

"Young girls," Rugg answered. "Preferably minors."

The taxista nodded. "Ah, menores. Qué bueno." The narrowed scope of Rugg's search seemed to rally him. "The young ones work in private clubs," he offered. "Not everyone can see them. I cannot see them. Only special customers enter. Perhaps you can try."

"Are there many?" Rugg asked.

"Girls?"

"Clubs."

"I know two. There are more, I think."

"Take me to the ones you know," Rugg said.

They drove. When Rugg asked about the customers who entered the clubs, the taxista said they were especially important or especially dangerous. Sometimes both. "They are men who answer but to God. The law is their whore."

The street where they parked was laid with paving stones. The taxista pointed to the curbed vehicles, some double-parked, others with drivers. Rugg took in the large, two-story house with a walled patio. Men entered and departed. He heard their curses, their liquored laughs. Rugg took out the mobile and dialed again, listening. He asked the taxista for the name of the neighborhood and the name of the street. "Are you certain young girls work here?"

The driver said his brother-in-law was a Pacífico route-man who regularly delivered beer to the house. "He has seen the girls. They are his daughter's age. His daughter will turn thirteen next month."

Rugg studied the house. "That is young," he said.

The driver nodded. "Do you wish to descend, mister?"

"Not tonight," Rugg said.

He cranked up his window before they drove past the house. The street frontage grassed, the entrance with wide wooden doors sentineled by a watchman. Rugg unable to see if he was armed.

Their second stop made in an outlying barrio at a brick-and-stucco house, the only masonry construction amid cobbled shanties. Rugg observed two cars parked on the dirt street. They waited. The taxista smoked. He told Rugg the police brought to the house adolescent runaways and homeless girls picked up on the streets. "It is a voiced secret. Men come here to buy and sell them."

No one came or went from the house. Rugg dialed once more, deciding the gavilleros would not bring his lovely daughter to such an abortive and unprofitable end. He let the phone ring until it didn't.

At the hotel the driver gave Rugg his card. "I'm at your service for whatever pleasure," he said. In the lobby Rugg found young Pedro asleep in the chair, the old man behind the front desk. "All clear, Mr. Rugg. No visitors. No calls." Rugg said they would breakfast on the street at eight. Then he ascended.

The room hot and smelling of Rugg's unwashed clothes. He lifted the window shade to check the street before he sat to remove the stripper clip from his ankle and to unwrap the leg dressing. He lay on the bed to consider what he had just seen and the likelihood that Rose worked in a private club and how to know which one and how to enter it without the credentials of a person especially important or especially dangerous who answered but to God.

How not to endanger her.

On the mobile he counted the calls made to her number. Almost a month since she was taken and he no closer now than that day. From under the bed he took the folder and removed her photo. He touched her face. No mother would forgive him, he reflected. Not her own, not any other. The old man had said it — she may have left the state. He had not said she may be dead, but what he had said the same as the end of the world revealed by mistake.

No place in Rugg to turn outside his sickened soul.

He returned the photo to the folder. The endangerment of his daughter a bomb countdown in reverse — her deliverance the only clock that ticked. He thought about the dirty cop from the highway stop and what he had said about bigger dogs, the ones that smelled blood. The cop's collaboration deemed perilous then. Now it seemed the lesser evil. If he was the one who had come to the hotel, soon the gavilleros would know.

Only one way to close the circle, Rugg decided. A way to find her if she was to be found.

Later he dozed with the gun on the bed.

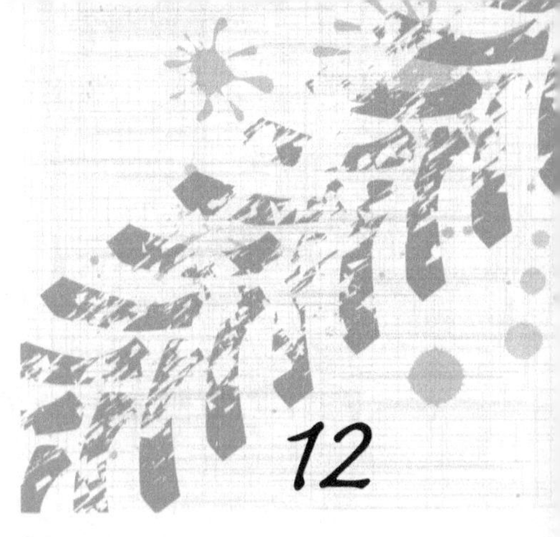

12

I've seen dead batos — mostly shot — but this is the first time
I see a dead bato without his head. We drive the highway
south of Los Toltecas. I'm in the back seat, looking out the
window. A pair of federal cops have already pulled over.
I recognize the big one who talks on his phone. He's the cop
who patrols the state line and the tollbooths at Estación Don.
He's the same one I saw in the girlie joint. The other cop I
don't recognize. He leans on the cruiser taking in the view,
like a dead bato isn't a big deal. Cachoro stops our ride behind
the cruiser. I hear him tell El Sin, "It's Tomás." Cachoro is
on a first-name basis with highway law enforcement because
his cousin is some top-dog federal cop. El Sin gets down.
I watch him walk up to the big cop, who ends his phone call
when he sees El Sin. They shake hands, exchange abrazos.

I look at the dead bato who lies in the breakdown lane.
His head is gone, and he's naked except for his undershorts,

which were white once. His hands and feet are bound with duct tape. His body is shot and stabbed. I look around for the bato's head, thinking it's been carried off, and then I see it on the highway fence. The head is stuck on one of the posts, like a stick pop. It's the head of a young bato who was trying to grow a mustache. His teeth are bared with a cigarette between them. The cigarette looks smoked. The bato's eyes are open and looking in my direction. I stare back. I've been trying to grow a mustache too. Our ride idles while El Sin and the big cop share some roadside laughs. I don't think they're talking about the dead bato.

Zuky says, "That Güero is crazy." I listen and keep my mouth shut. I know only one Güero who is crazy — Güero del Café. Cachoro asks, "What's with the cigarette? Cali didn't smoke." Zuky shrugs. "I told you. He's crazy. Another motherless job." It's an earful, but now I know the name of the headless bato. He's the celebrated Cali — the car thief who stepped on El Sin's turf — the bato who dodged our roadblocks in Guasave. I figured Cali for an old bato, but he's new. I stare at his head, getting a first-hand look at the knife work of Güero del Café. A motherless job seen close up is not the same as hearing about it. I watch El Sin and the big cop chat. They look at something on the cop's phone. When the morgue van arrives, the cop and El Sin shake hands, and El Sin returns to our ride. The big cop points the morgue workers to the fence. One of them puts on gloves before he fetches the head. He holds it by the hair, like the Indians do when they take scalps in the Old West movies. As we pull away, I see the cop taking pictures of Cali — the body and the head. Cachoro accelerates onto the highway.

El Sin turns around and looks at Zuky, who sits beside me. "Was the gringo dead?" he asks out of nowhere. I know better than to look at Zuky. I look out the window. The first gringo that pops into my head is the badass gringo, daddy of the gringa in the girlie joint. Zuky says, "What gringo?" El Sin says, "The last one." Our crew sits quiet. Everyone waits for Zuky to remember. Then he nods. "Oh yeah. We got him." El Sin asks, "Did you finish him?" I feel Zuky shift in the seat. "No, Güero did," he answers. When El Sin asks if he saw the Güero finish the gringo, Zuky replies, "I saw what he cut. The gringo was done. Ask Fer." El Sin faces front. I see him check his phone. No one speaks. We drive a while before Zuky says, "What's the stink anyway?" El Sin answers, "No stink." Then Zuky asks, "But why did you ask if he was dead?" It's the same question I ask myself. How could the gringo be alive if Güero del Café finished him? No one outruns that drugged devil. El Sin turns around again. His face has that scary, no-face look he had when he shot the mustached bato. "That's my business," he says. "Next time finish yours." Zuky shifts again. It's good to see him squirm, but it's scary to see El Sin when his face has nothing on it. If he thinks the gringo is alive, he didn't hear it from anyone in our ride. Most likely he heard it from the big cop. The one called Tomás.

Seeing is believing when there's news of the dead walking. And if the news comes from a cop, I'd believe a blind man first. I wonder if El Sin will send someone to find the gringo's body. I wonder if Zuky isn't done squirming. I wonder if Güero kept the gringo's toes. There's a lot to wonder about, which is not always better than having nothing to wonder about.

The cut-off head of Cali comes back to me, his underfed mustache. I'm not shaving mine yet. A mustache makes me look older and tougher, which is how I want to look.

THEY BREAKFASTED AT A birria stand frequented by Pedro for its handmade tortillas. Rugg took the last of the antibiotics before he paid. Then he told Pedro to drive him to the Federal Police headquarters.

"Are you sure, Mr. Rugg?"

"Sure."

The comandancia occupied an unpainted block building topped with towered antennas. It sat off the highway and adjacent to a fenced area that held vehicle wrecks and impoundments. Rugg read the call numbers on the cruisers parked in the spaces at the front of the building. He did not see the cruiser from the road stop.

He told Pedro to wait in the truck. "It is better," he said.

"I'm not afraid of rats, big or small," the old man replied.

"I know."

He crutched with the folder in his hand. Inside, he stood before a false wall cut with a windowed opening for public ministration. Behind the window and below its sill sat a woman who did not take notice of Rugg until he spoke. He asked to see the commander.

"He's out," she answered.

Rugg inquired if he was out of the office or out of the city.

"Out," she repeated.

Rugg said he would wait.

When the woman asked his business, Rugg said his business was with the commander or with the officer in charge.

She looked at Rugg. "If you wish to file a complaint, you must see the public prosecutor downtown."

Rugg said he had not come to file a complaint but to report an accident.

"What kind of accident?"

"I will report that to the person in charge."

The woman rose from where she sat, her head reaching the window. She saw Rugg's crutches. "Is this a highway accident?" she asked.

"It is related."

Rugg stood without his cap.

"Are you a tourist?"

"Yes."

"One moment."

Rugg set the folder on the sill and shifted his weight onto the crutches. He knew a moment could take longer than any known increment of time. No chairs available in the narrow room. The walls bare except for a police insignia painted above the door and captioned with a motto that Rugg read without adjudication: Proteger y Servir a la Comunidad. He saw no reward posters for the hunted or the missing. No one else entered the room.

The man who appeared at the window was clean-shaven. His hair oiled and combed. He wore a uniform with gold stars on the shoulder straps. "How may I be of service?" he began.

Rugg said he wished to speak in private, if the moment was not inopportune.

The officer not much younger than Rugg. Etched on his face the years of a cop. His gaze measured Rugg before he nodded. "You must go to the back to enter," he instructed.

At the rear of the comandancia Rugg found the steel security door ajar. He crutched into a corridor and past cubicle offices occupied by uniformed and nonuniformed men, some at desks, others grouped in conversation. They looked at him. The officer met Rugg and led him to a windowless office with metal file cabinets, a small desk, and two armless plastic chairs. "Please sit," he said.

Rugg sat. He held the crutches at his side. The folder he set on his lap. He asked the man if he was the commander.

"Comandante Magaña, at your orders. With whom do I have the pleasure?"

"Rugg. Bob Rugg."

The commander inquired how he could help. Rugg opened the folder and held out the photograph of Rose. "My daughter," he said.

Commander Magaña took it.

"Her name is Rose," Rugg said. "She is thirteen."

"Thirteen?"

"Yes. My only daughter."

"Your Spanish is good, Mr. Rugg. I confess my English is not."

Rugg took back the photo. He told the commander about losing Rose to the masked highway gavilleros, about losing his leg, his truck, his passport. He watched the commander's face. It said such stories were not new to him.

"Where did this happen?" he asked.

"South of the tollplaza at Estación Don." Rugg did not offer the kilometer marker. When the commander asked the time of the assault, Rugg gave the day and the hour. He observed an HK rifle leaning on the file cabinet nearest the desk. The weapon held a plastic Magpul magazine with a viewing window through which Rugg saw the rounds left to be fired.

"You have been recuperating in the hospital, Mr. Rugg?"

"Yes. Until recently."

"And you have not reported the incident?"

Rugg said he had waited for his daughter's photo and other documents to arrive.

The commander nodded. "Of course. Were there other occupants in the vehicle?"

"No."

"Witnesses?"

"None that will come forward."

When the commander asked what Rugg meant, he said that a large truck had halted briefly on the highway before continuing its route.

"The driver lent no assistance?"

Rugg shook his head. He did not say that the presence of armed men on the highway had likely discouraged assistance.

"You said the men were masked?"

"All but one. He was in charge."

"Please describe him."

"Not a young man," Rugg said. "He had silver hair, close-cropped in a military cut. He spoke English."

"English?"

"Fluent."

Commander Magaña took no notes. He looked plainly at Rugg. "Even thieves surprise us with their skills," he observed.

Rugg said the boss was no common thief.

"Would you recognize him if you saw him again?"

Rugg said, "I would know him inside a coon's ass."

The coinage foreign to the commander. "Excuse me?"

"In the dark I would know him," Rugg said.

The commander nodded. "That is good. I must remember it. And what of the other thieves? Did any stand out?"

Rugg described the teenage boy who wore sneakers and walked with a limp. "After he took my wallet, he winked at me. His mask was cut from a sock hat."

"You have a good memory, Mr. Rugg. I'm impressed. Do you remember how you got from the highway to the hospital?"

Rugg said he had no recollection. He said the gavilleros had left him in the desert and later he woke up in the hospital with his leg amputated.

"So they shot you and left you?"

"Yes."

"Did they think you were dead?"

"I don't know what they thought."

"Of course."

When Rugg asked if the police dispatch logs had a record of an emergency call on that day, Commander Magaña said he would check. Rugg repeated the date and time of the assault. The commander did not rise from his chair.

"You said they stole your passport and wallet?"

"The passport went with the truck."

"You carry no identification, Mr. Rugg?"

From his back pocket Rugg removed the new wallet. He took out the replica license, handing it to the commander.

The commander examined both sides. "Robert Rugg. I see your name is not spelled like the carpet."

"No."

"You are a pilot?"

"Retired."

"Ah. Did you fly big planes?"

"Some."

"In the wars?"

"The forest service."

"And what do you do now?"

"I stay at home, except when I travel."

"Another question, Mr. Rugg. Where is the girl's mother?"

Rugg said she died two years before.

"I'm sorry. So you were traveling alone with your daughter?"

"I said there were no other occupants in the truck."

"You did. And what did you say your destination was?"

"I didn't. It was Mazatlán."

"Ah. The beach. Just the two of you. That is nice. A vacation."

Rugg said nothing. His gaze locked on the man's face. No looking away from a snake that lifted its head.

"We will need the information on your truck, of course. You may provide it in your formal complaint, along with copies of the vehicle registration and title."

"I don't care about the truck. I want my daughter."

The commander smiled. "Naturally. The information is a means to an end. If we find your truck, it may lead us to your daughter."

"I doubt it."

When the commander asked who would have seen Rugg and his daughter together that day, Rugg said every tollplaza operator on the southbound lanes of Highway

15 between Nogales and the Sonoran border, and the gasoline dispatchers and the window wipes at the Pemex stations on the Empalme loop and in downtown Navojoa, and the woman who served them breakfast in the Café Elba in Santa Ana, and the cashier at the same café who offered his daughter a wrapped sweet from the candy bowl next to the cash register, and the man in the café parking lot who bucket-washed his truck while they breakfasted, and the gavilleros themselves, who numbered a dozen, give or take a gunman. Rugg said those were the ones he remembered, though there were others he could not name who had witnessed their journey.

"That is sufficient," the commander said.

Rugg stood the crutches between his legs. "Why do you ask?"

Commander Magaña said he was trying to sort out the details of a journey made by a father and a teenage girl during which the father is shot but not killed, the girl vanishes, there are no witnesses, and the police are notified by the father a month after the occurrence. "I am trying to understand it," he said.

"Stop the cart. My daughter didn't vanish. She was abducted. Are you suggesting I had something to do with it?" Rugg was dismayed with himself for not having seen this train around the bend.

"No, Mr. Rugg. I am simply playing it out in the public eye, as it were. You brought your daughter to Mexico, where something bad happened to her, where you were unable to protect her, which is the extent of your involvement, I'm sure. And now you come to me."

"I was in the hospital. Then I waited for my documents. Why don't you check your dispatch logs for that day? There should be a report of a gringo shot on the highway."

"There are no reports, Mr. Rugg. A tourist's misfortunes in my jurisdiction do not pass unperceived. I would not mislead you on this. Perhaps the Ministerial Police have a report. Did anyone from that office come to the hospital to question you?"

"Not while I was awake."

"They have much overdue work, as do we. I recommend you begin by filing a formal complaint with the public prosecutor, so that an investigation may be opened, and the corresponding agencies alerted. A case that involves a shooting, a robbery, and an abduction merits our highest priority. Have you returned to the scene, Mr. Rugg?"

Rugg said he had not.

The commander handed back the license. "You will need this," he said. "Please gather your daughter's specifics. Her height and weight, a record of any scars or piercings. A copy of her passport would be helpful. Your filing should include her most recent photo. Does she have a tattoo?"

"No."

"Are you sure, Mr. Rugg? Often a parent is the last one to know these things."

"I know."

He studied Rugg. "Have you informed your consulate in Hermosillo?"

Rugg said he had not.

"They may be of assistance with documents. My advice is to call them."

"I will," Rugg said. "Where do I look for her?"

Commander Magaña shook his head. "Let us look for her, Mr. Rugg."

"Where will you look for her?"

The commander folded his hands. "Unfortunately, the abduction of a teenage girl is complicated. I won't get into details, but there are many places to look. Is it possible she returned to the United States?"

He shook his head. "Her passport was in the truck."

"How about family? Could she have contacted a relative?"

Rugg said he would have heard.

"Of course. Nevertheless, please include family names and contact information in your complaint. Do you need directions to the public prosecutor's office?"

Not how Rugg had intended to walk this tightrope. The man's charade without end. "I'm not doing that," he said.

"Excuse me?"

"I'm not filing."

"Mr. Rugg, we need a written complaint to begin our investigation."

"No, you don't. You need my cooperation, which I'm prepared to offer."

Commander Magaña unfolded his hands in inquiry. "I do not understand."

"Do you know of this man?" he asked.

"What man?"

"The one I described. The man who abducted my daughter."

"How would I know him, Mr. Rugg? He is a criminal."

"I asked if you know of him, the way cops know of criminals, their associates and hideouts."

The commander shook his head. "I know of many, and many know of me. The man you describe could be one of the many, or he could be none of them."

"You skate well," Rugg said. "Even where the ice is thin."

"I'm sorry. As I said, I do not know much English."

"I said I will pay you to find her. In a private capacity."

Rugg watched his face; nothing given up. How cop vigilance hid behind an earnest gaze.

"Please, Mr. Rugg. There is no need. It is my job. You are too desperate, I think."

"Two hundred thousand pesos for her safe return," Rugg offered. "Half up front. Half when I have her. Cash."

The thin curl of the commander's lips the same as a serpent's smile — if nature had gifted lips to serpents. "You are a traveled man, my friend. You know it is a serious crime to offer money to a policeman."

"Think of it as a reward." Rugg said.

"You cannot find your daughter from jail. The penalties for subornation are severe."

"I'm not worried about penalties."

"But you should be. I am the last honest cop in Mexico, Mr. Rugg."

"Honest bullshit."

The commander smiled. "One English word I do know."

Rugg shifted the crutches. "And I know there are men who know where abducted girls are taken. I know these men charge for information."

The commander said he was not one of those men.

"Fifty thousand for the boss," Rugg offered. "Name, place, and no interference."

"Is that a reward too?"

"A bounty," Rugg rejoined.

Commander Magaña shrugged. "I must refuse both offers, and I will try to forget that you made them. For the sake of your daughter."

Rugg asked for a paper and a pen. He wrote down his mobile number, the name of the hotel, and his room number. He placed the paper and pen on the desk in front of the commander before he retook the crutches and stood with the folder in his hand. "Should you change your mind," he said. "For the sake of my daughter."

The commander gazed at the paper. "Very well, Mr. Rugg. Do you carry an extra photo of her? I will post it on our bulletin board to advance the search."

Rugg said he had brought only the one.

"Allow me to make a copy." The commander took the photo and left the office. Rugg stood by the desk. He heard distant voices, the sound of a copy machine. His gaze fell on the HK rifle that leaned against the filing cabinet. A weapon he had fired in combat. The commander returned with the photo.

Rugg took it. "You should know that the Magpul magazine doesn't have an anti-tilt follower," he said.

Commander Magaña followed Rugg's gaze to the rifle.

"… The follower in that model jams before the last rounds empty."

The commander looked at him and smiled. "You know guns, Mr. Rugg?"

Rugg said he knew what he read.

"Then you have read much, I think. Fortunately, that is not my weapon, but one that belonged to a man who died shooting it. A bad man, I must add. Bad, but also a good shot. He killed two of my men with it. And you are right. The rifle jammed, and then he was shot dead by me. Later the rifle came to my office, where I keep it out of remembrance for the fallen officers. The rounds you see through the viewing window were intended for me, for my brain, because the weapon was pointed at my head when it jammed. It is still jammed, and I've left it so to remind me how luck plays largely in our lives and in our deaths. You know something of this, Mr. Rugg. You were left for dead but did not die. This fortuity allows you to look for your daughter. And thank you for telling me why this rifle jammed. It is reassuring to know that our fortunes derive from a specific cause."

Rugg nodded. Then he told the commander what he had saved for last, should the offer of a reward be rebuffed. He said he just remembered that two days earlier, a Federal Police officer had visited the hotel asking for a gringo. Rugg explained that he was out at the time, but the desk clerk had described the officer as a big man. "He did not leave his name, but perhaps he works for you." Rugg watched the commander grip the unforeseen and put it far from his face with a smile.

"Perhaps he was from another agency," he replied.

"Perhaps," Rugg said. "Perhaps he is investigating another gringo at the hotel. I'm glad I remembered to tell you."

"I'm sure it was routine. Thank you."

Rugg crutched to the door. Outside, he found the old man eating chips from a bag opened days before.

"How did it go?"

"I hit the hive," Rugg answered.

Pedro offered the bag to Rugg. The chips stale.

They drove, Rugg telling the old man that the search for his daughter had advanced too far for him to move to another hotel without losing what might be gained by staying where he was. He said he would pay young Pedro and Carlos their full wages to suspend their front desk duties for the next days, that it was best for them not to be at the hotel should troublesome visitors arrive.

The old man understood. "Bees, Mr. Rugg?"

"Bees."

Pedro offered to man the desk. His brother, he said, would be glad to save the wages.

Rugg told him that caution was imperative. "Cops can be more dangerous than criminals."

The old man asked if they would lead him to Rose.

"We'll see," Rugg said.

At the hotel he instructed Pedro to park the Ranger behind the building.

I go to my aunt's house, where I get a smile and a hug. She doesn't call me a good-for-nothing anymore — not since I started giving her money instead of stealing it. Now she's happy to see me. "Sit," she says. "Eat." She feeds me a plate of meat and beans, which is more filling than the old menu of tortillas with salt. She knows I'm up to no good, but she doesn't ask me what I do or where I go or how I get my cash because both of us eat off my pesos. The dead Macho Prieto was right when he said money makes up for who you aren't. To my aunt I'm finally someone.

I don't show her the Colt. I leave it in my pack, which I carry with clothes from the crash house. I go to the latrine, where I change, and when I return to the house, I lay a two-hundred-peso bill on the kitchen table. My aunt puts it in her apron, and she says, "Gracias, hijo." She calls me son ever since I started giving her money. It has a false *ring, but I'm not complaining. Before I leave, she gives me another hug and tells me to go with God, whatever that means.*

IN LARGE PRINT Rugg wrote ABDUCTED at the top of her photo. At the bottom he wrote Rose's name and her date of birth. He added: "For Eric White, US Consulate. From Bob Rugg." He dialed the number into the telefax on the card table.

The old man stood by. Earlier, he had sent Carlos home. Pedrito had been given the night off.

"Are you sure you want me to do nothing?"

Rugg nodded. He had instructed the old man to remain behind the desk that night, preferably seated and under his cap. Hotel guests, he had advised, should be lodged on the second floor. He had further instructed Pedro to volunteer Rugg's room number, if enjoined to do so, but to otherwise keep his head down and say nothing.

"These men are careful," Rugg said. "If they come, if they find what they expect to find — a dead hotel, a mum clerk — they will likely go upstairs, which is where I want to meet them, for your safety and for Rose's."

Pedro admitted that silence wasn't his don, but that he would shut up for Rose.

After the fax cleared, Rugg waited before he dialed the consulate number and the line extension for Eric

White. He leaned on the counter, the pain large in his leg. When a man's voice answered, Rugg asked if he had gotten the fax.

"Is this Mr. Rugg?"

"Yeah. Did you get my fax?"

"Yes. Thank you for getting back to me. I'm Eric White, a consular officer. I called several times, but the hotel told me you were no longer at this number."

Rugg said he had returned. He asked that his daughter's abduction be reported to Mexican law enforcement, and that her photo be added to their database. "That's why I called."

"Of course. Have you alerted the local police?"

"I have. They have not found her."

The consular officer said he needed additional information.

"Shoot," Rugg said.

"OK. Just a minute."

Rugg heard keyboard strokes. Eric White cleared his voice. "So, what was the time and date of the abduction?"

"Your duty officer took down that information. I don't have time to repeat it."

A pause. More keyboard strokes. "Yes, I have it. OK. Estación Don, Sonora, on the twenty-third. Got it."

Rugg waited.

"What is Rose's height and weight?"

Rugg gave his best guess.

"Hair color?"

"Blond."

"Eyes?"

"Blue."

"I apologize, Mr. Rugg. The faxed photo is black and white. Does she have any scars, piercings, or tattoos?"

"No."

"Is there a life-threatening medical condition that we should add to the alert?"

"She was abducted."

"I understand, but one that is specifically medical. For example, is there a medication she must have."

The pill of hope, Rugg thought. "No," he said.

"Do you recall what she was wearing?"

Rugg described her clothes. He said she was taken without shoes."

"Does she speak Spanish?"

"No."

"Is there someone she might contact in Mexico?"

"No."

"How about Rose's mother? Has she been notified?"

Rugg explained.

"I'm sorry. It's a question we must ask. You are the custodial parent, then?"

"Yes."

When Rugg said he wanted his mobile listed on the alert, the consular officer replied that the consulate emergency telephone was the only number allowed, for tracking purposes. "But let me take your number."

His patience kept for Rose. He dictated the number.

"We discourage the family from negotiating directly with the abductors or pursuing any extralegal avenues that could jeopardize a favorable outcome."

Rugg said nothing.

"Do you have kidnapping insurance, Mr. Rugg?"

"No. Would that have helped?" He heard the keyboard strokes stop.

"Not directly. I bring it up because the alert can include the mention of a reward. Or not."

"Include it."

"OK. It's a simple advisory: 'Reward for information leading to the safe return.' No sum is specified."

Rugg waited.

"That's all we need for your daughter. The alert will be sent to the Mexican federal and state agencies and to US law enforcement. Customs and border patrol agents will be notified as well."

Rugg said he did not foresee his daughter reaching the border.

The consular officer replied that anything was possible. He said that, in a recent abduction, the victim had escaped her captors in Mazatlán and had returned by bus to Nogales, where she was recognized by a customs agent.

Rugg listened. Rose not so resourceful, he thought. He told the consul that he needed guidance on where to search. "Are most girls found in the state where they are abducted?"

"Let the police search, Mr. Rugg."

"Are they found alive?"

"I don't have the numbers, sir. Each case is different."

"The sex trade? Is that where these girls go?"

Silence from the consul.

"No need to sugarcoat it," Rugg said.

"I encourage you to avoid speculation. The report says you were shot. Are you getting treatment?"

Rugg said he was fine. "If I get Rose on a flight to Hermosillo, can you have someone meet her at the airport and get her to the consulate?"

"Of course."

The consul covered his handset to speak to someone else. Rugg checked his watch.

"Mr. Rugg, did you file a stolen vehicle report?"

"No."

"We need the vehicle description and the VIN to issue a bulletin."

"I don't need the vehicle," Rugg said. "I bought another."

"Should it turn up, it may provide a lead."

"Don't hold your breath."

"Excuse me?"

Rugg said he had to go. "You have my cell. I'll try to pick up."

"Mr. Rugg ..."

He crutched to the lobby chair. The old man brought a glass of water. "Much talk," he said.

"Diplomats," Rugg replied. He stared through the streetfront glass. Done, he thought. The dice thrown at this last resort. World alerted. Reward offered. Soon the cops would learn that others knew of Rose and gringo money, the biggest dogs likely to outrun the small ones. He asked the old man if he was ready.

"I'm with you one hundred on this. But why don't you wait in the lobby?"

The room was less public, Rugg explained.

"I could signal if they come."

Rugg said no signal was needed. He told the old man that should he depart with the visitors and not reappear tomorrow, it was likely he would not return. "In which case," Rugg said, "dispose of the items in my room. Keep the Ranger."

The old man reseated his Dodgers cap. "But you'll need it to drive out Rose."

Rugg told him that he would make other arrangements, that the truck was a liability on the highway. He opened his wallet and handed Pedro the bills inside. "Gas money," he said. He rose from the chair. "Remember, stay behind the desk, no matter what." Then Rugg ascended the stairs.

In the room he dropped the window shade and lowered himself to the floor to remove the handgun and the stripper clip from where he had taped them to the bedframe. He retrieved the bundled money, counting the bills before he rebundled them. Enough cash to parley, he decided. With the duct tape he fastened the bundles into a packet and put it under the blanket at the foot of the bed. He fashioned a second stripper clip from the remaining cartridges in the box and taped it to his leg. The first clip he taped across his abdomen above the belt. He checked his watch. It was time to let her know.

Sue answered on the first ring. Rugg said he had only a minute.

"I deserve more than that. Why haven't you called?"

"I've been busy. A long story."

"You said that before. Where's Rose? Put her on."

No dance left in him. "I can't," he said. "She's been taken."

"Taken? Taken where?"

"I don't know."

"What? Is she …?"

"No. Abducted. She was taken by the men who car-jacked the truck."

"You said she was with you."

"I know."

"Where is she, goddamn it? You told me she was fine, and now you say she's abducted. What the hell, Bob!"

"Calm down. It's almost over. I'm negotiating her release."

"Her release? She's been missing all this time? Do you know if she's OK?"

"I know."

"How do you know? Have you spoken to her?"

"Not yet."

"Christ, Bob. Make them put her on the phone. You need to get someone who knows how to handle this. Did they say how much they want?"

Rugg said he needed twenty thousand dollars.

His sister repeated the amount, her voice in uppercase. "Make them put her on the phone. What about the police? What are they doing?"

"They're involved."

Silence.

"You need a negotiating expert, Bob. I've read about Mexican police."

"Sue. Send the money. Send it in two transfers to the same Western Union as before, but in my name. You have the information."

"Please get a professional. There are people in the State Department who know. Did you call the consulate number?"

"I did."

"What did they say?"

Rugg said they had sent out an alert with Rose's photograph to the law enforcement agencies in both countries. "They have your contact information."

Dead air. He waited for her to say something.

"That's why you wanted her picture. You sonofabitch, Bob."

"Things hadn't sorted out yet. I thought it best."

"You said you were shot. Is that true?"

"Yes."

"I don't know what to believe. This isn't fair. A thirteen-year-old girl who lost her mother. You couldn't stop them?"

"I tried."

"Jesus, Bob."

"I'll bring her back."

"I don't want to think about what they might do. I told you that you shouldn't take her."

"You did."

"Should I call Randy?"

"Who?"

"Randy. The Marine recruiter I met. Maybe he knows people who can go down there."

"Not now, Sue. Text me the transfer numbers. Here's my mobile."

"Your mobile? You have a phone and you didn't call me?"

Rugg read the number. "Remember: Two transfers in my name. Text me the confirmations."

"I got it the first time. Where are you staying? What hotel?"

"San Carlos. It's small."

She repeated it as though to herself. "The San Carlos in Los Mochis."

Rugg heard her cover the handset. "Sue?"

"Don't say it."

"Sue. It's OK. I'll bring her back. I've got to go."

Her muffled weeping.

"Sue. Please. Can you drive to Lawton now?"

Sniffles. Silence. "Yes."

"Thanks. I'll call when I have her, OK?"

"You better."

"OK. 'Bye."

"Hold her for me, Bob."

"I will."

After he hung up, he switched the mobile to vibrate and pocketed the phone. He folded one of his socks and wedged it between the door and the jamb opposite the hinges. The door left unlocked. The roll of duct tape he set on the nightstand. He dragged the chair to the window and sat with the bed pillow on his lap, the window shade lifted enough to view the street. The gun rested on his lap. He knew they might not show. Men's greed as incalculable as their bounty.

14

It's early, the street still gray when I reach the meet point. "You're late," Zuky says. "We got a job." The ride is a black Cherokee we boosted days before on the coast highway. Zuky is alone. I climb in and ask, "What job?" He says, "A job job, dumbass. Are you driving?" That's normal Zuky talk. He drives. I look out the window, not seeing much. Zuky asks if I brought the pistol. When I say it's in my pack, he tells me to show it. I pull out the Colt. He asks if it's loaded, and I tell him it is. "Wear it," he says. I stick the Colt under my belt, and he asks what else is in the pack. I tell him a box of rounds, my mask, and clothes. He takes the pack and throws it in the back seat. Then he tells me to hand over my phone, which I do. "I'm keeping it," he says. Zuky seems spooked, but I know better than to say so.

We pull over on a street, and he points to a building across from where we parked. "Stay and watch it," he says. The *building has a hotel sign but no name. The sign is lit. The place looks familiar, and then I remember it's the hotel where I clocked the fat bato who came regular every morning, like he was the owner. It was my first job birding a bato. I tell Zuky, "You mean the fat guy?" He says, "No, dumbass, the gringo." I don't hide my surprise. "The gringo?" Zuky spits out the window. "Are you deaf? You heard Sin jam me in the car." I remember it — Zuky was the dumbass then. "Didn't you say he was dead?" I ask. Zuky doesn't answer straightaway. He looks at the hotel. "¡Que chingue a su madre el Güero!" he snaps. I know to keep my mouth shut. Mother insults are best ignored if they're not about your own mother. He looks at me and says, "Sin wants you to watch for him. So watch!" I nod. It's the second time Zuky calls our boss Sin instead of El Sin — which is how we call him, for respect.*

Zuky opens the Cherokee's console and pulls out a flip phone and tosses it on my lap. "His ride is a white Ranger, no plates. Call if he shows." I put the phone in my pocket. "So, he's not dead?" I ask, just to be sure. Zuky cusses and calls me a dumbass again, and he tells me that if the gringo has a ride, how can he be dead. I get out of the car and pull my shirt over the Colt. Zuky says, "The gringo is missing a foot. He's on crutches. Even a dumbass can spot him." I nod. The Cherokee idles at the curb. Then Zuky says, "I call you dumbass because I think you're OK. So don't take it personal, dumbass." He doesn't look at me. He looks out the front glass. "Maybe you'll work for me someday," he says.

I nod again, though it sounds weird, working for Zuky. "What if he leaves?" I ask. Zuky gives me the old glare. "Leaves?" he repeats. I lean into the window to keep my voice down. "Yeah. What if the gringo leaves?" I see Zuky move the shift lever. "Shoot him, dumbass. He's on crutches. We'll finish." The Cherokee starts to roll. I pull my head out of the window before he steps on the gas and nearly runs over my good foot.

RUGG DID NOT SEE when they entered from the street, but he heard their footfalls on the stairs. The old man's voice not heard. He sat facing the door, the pillow held over the Smith & Wesson, the room left dark.

Their shadows fell across the light beneath the door. Two shadows. Possibly three. He heard the handle rotate. When they pushed the door, the wedged sock held it. In their stilled shadows the hesitation of men who stood before an unlocked door that didn't open. Cops, he guessed. One of them spoke. "Señor Rugg. Soy Comandante Magaña."

Rugg waited.

"Señor Rugg?"

Rugg called out that the door was unlocked.

The commander spoke in a low voice to another. Aloud, he asked, "Are you armed, Mr. Rugg?"

"Push the door," Rugg said. "It's open."

"We come to talk. Are you armed?"

"No."

Hallway light spilled into the room when the door opened. Rugg a dim figure seated in the corner. The commander stood to one side of the doorway, where the frame provided cover. The other visitor unseen, a silhouette drawn largely on the far wall.

"Your daughter's safe return is our priority," the commander said.

Rugg nodded. "At two in the morning."

"Do you not want her back at any hour, Mr. Rugg?"

"I do. Who came with you?"

"Another investigator."

The silhouette unmoved.

"You mean backup."

"May I enter, Mr. Rugg?"

Under the pillow, Rugg kept the pistol leveled at the door. He asked the commander to show himself fully, hands first.

"Mr. Rugg, is this necessary?"

"It's business, Commander. I have something you want. You have something I want. What neither of us wants is trouble."

The commander stepped into the doorway and showed his hands. He stood in civilian attire, his weapon concealed. The other appeared behind him. Rugg recognized the big cop from the highway stop.

"Buenas noches, Señor Rugg," he greeted. "¿Se acuerda de mí?"

Rugg said he not only remembered him, he remembered the ten thousand pesos extorted when they last met.

The big cop out of uniform. He smiled. "Are you still a tourist with no papers?"

"I am. Are you still a cop with no integrity?"

The smile faded. His eyes checked the hallway.

"Mr. Rugg, we did not come to exchange insults," the commander said.

"I know. You came to rob me. Who else is with you?"

The commander said that only he and the officer had come.

"What about the lobby?"

"No one. And we did not come to rob. We came to assist."

"Right." Rugg told the big cop to put his weapon on the floor and push it past the door.

The cop said he carried no weapon.

"Bullshit."

They looked to where Rugg sat in the corner.

"Sáquela," Rugg repeated. He raised the Smith & Wesson from under the pillow.

The commander nodded to the officer. The big cop removed the weapon from his backside. He placed it on the floor and slid it across the tile. Rugg saw it was a machine pistol with a sound suppressor.

Rugg told the commander to advance. He told the big cop not to move. "I'll shoot you first."

Commander Magaña stepped into the room. "You said you were not armed."

"I lied. Lay your weapon on the floor."

The commander opened his jacket. The weapon a compact holstered on his left shoulder.

"Use the other hand," Rugg warned.

After Magaña drew it and set it on the floor, Rugg told him to take the blanket off the bed and throw it over the weapons. Then he told him to sit on the bed. The big cop he told to sit on the floor and cross his legs.

The cop called it an insult. Rugg said that for a big man he was easily insulted. He told the cop to do as instructed or his dead mother would see him without a bath.

He sat. "Be careful what you say about my mother, gringo. I know things you don't want to know. I saw your daughter's picture at the comandancia."

Rugg pointed to the bundled cash on the bed. "Good-faith money, Commander. When my daughter is safe, I pay the rest."

Commander Magaña took the bundle. "This does not feel like one hundred thousand pesos."

"I said, good-faith money. One hundred thousand pesos is not a sum a traveler keeps in a hotel room when his guests are crooked cops."

"Nothing is gained by these insults," the commander replied. "I thought we had an arrangement."

"You turned it down, Commander, back when you were the last honest cop in Mexico. This is the new deal. That's thirty in the bundle. After my daughter is on a flight to Hermosillo, we will go to the telegraph office for the balance, which is one-hundred-and-seventy-thousand pesos, less the ten thousand I gave this bandit."

"Wait a moment," interjected the big cop.

"Shut up," Rugg said.

The commander shook his head. "How do we know you will pay us?"

"You have thirty. I have nothing. Who is trusting who? I'm still in your country."

"And if I don't accept?"

Rugg said he would take back the thirty and they could leave without their weapons, that he would not shoot them until the next time he saw them.

The commander and the big cop exchanged glances.

"We are not the only ones who know where to find you, Mr. Rugg. The men who took your daughter and left you for dead, they know you are alive."

"Good," Rugg said. "I will make them an offer when they come."

The big cop guffawed. "You should have left Mexico. It is too late for you now. You are a dead gringo."

Rugg ignored him. He told the commander that his daughter's abduction had been bulletined to other police agencies. "Perhaps someone will come forward for the reward."

The commander said no cop would seek the reward, because no reward was worth his life and the lives of his family.

"We'll see," Rugg said. "You came. That's a start."

"I came because you sought my assistance."

Rugg gestured toward the door. "Go, Commander. Take the bandit. Leave the weapons."

The big cop grinned. "I showed them your picture, gringo. I was there when the Red Cross brought your shot carcass to the road. I took photos. Do you want to see them? They're on my phone."

Rugg told him not to reach for his pocket.

"I called the ambulance. I bagged your watch and ring. You're alive because of me."

"Alive enough to shoot you," Rugg said.

"When I stopped you on the road, I knew you looked familiar. It's amazing how warm blood and a missing foot alter the semblance of a man. You should have stayed dead. The boss himself is coming for you."

Rugg told the commander to leave before he changed his mind about shooting them.

"That old man downstairs," continued the big cop. "I remember him too. He was your driver."

"You have a bad memory, cop."

"Do I? No license. Wears huaraches. That cap. I'll make sure the boss knows the old fool helped you. He'll be next. They'll trash this little hotel."

Rugg thought about how a man could say too much and not have the sense to know where it could end.

The commander did not rise from the bed. "Mr. Rugg, I have reconsidered," he said. "We will take you to your daughter."

In Rugg's pocket his mobile vibrated. "The deal is, you get us to the airport. I put her on a flight. Then we go for the money."

Commander Magaña nodded. "You do not intend to depart with your daughter?"

"What comes after I pay you is my business." Rugg pointed to the bundled money. "Count it."

"There is no need."

Rugg told the big cop to put his phone on the floor and push it into the room. "Slowly."

"Why should I?" he said.

"Because I will put a hole in you if you don't."

"I need my phone, gringo. My wife is pregnant."

"Then you have two reasons not to be stupid."

The big cop complied. Rugg asked the commander to leave his phone on the bed.

"Mr. Rugg, I have police business …"

"Not tonight."

Rugg told the big cop to stand and turn around and put his hands behind his back, palms out. He instructed the commander to take the duct tape from the nightstand and secure the cop's wrists.

"You whoremothering son-of-a-fornication," the big cop barked. "You think you are going to hostage two cops. You on one foot."

"I do."

The commander rose from the bed and took the tape. "Mr. Rugg, this is a big mistake."

"Not the biggest by far," Rugg said. He watched him wrap the cop's wrists. "Tighter," he said. When the wrists were bound, he told the commander to tape the cop's hands back-to-back between the thumbs.

"I had your daughter, gringo," the big cop said over his shoulder. "I had her. She's a skimpy whore with no tits and a mole the color of a cherry on her white ass. Check my phone."

Rugg's silence sucked into a shriveled moment, remembrance jarred, the fragile recollection shattered, how he had first seen his naked newborn Rose asleep in her crib, his wife pointing at the cherry birthmark, his birthmark, the blessing of nature. Of all possible obscenities grossly uttered, this beyond what he had foreseen. Rugg's grip tightened on the pistol. He aimed at the big cop's head, where he saw the man's last thought and memory shredded. He told the commander to tape the cop's mouth.

"Those ten thousand pesos you gave me, gringo. I bought a night with her. You paid me to screw your own daughter."

The commander tore off a strip of tape and fixed it over the cop's mouth. The big cop grunted and snuffled. He faced Rugg. His eyes laughed.

"He is full of exaggeration," the commander explained.

Rugg said nothing. With the pistol he motioned for the commander to clear the doorway.

The big cop watched him. When Rugg reached for the crutches, he did not remove his gaze from the cop. He stood, holding the pistol to the crutch handgrip. "Don't think I'm not a good shot," he said. He told the commander to keep the tape and to move into the hallway.

Rugg crutched to where the blanket lay on the floor. With the crutch tip he folded it back, and he stooped to retrieve the weapons, his gaze steadied on the cops. The compact he slipped into his pocket. The machine pistol he stuck under his belt. They watched him. Rugg raised the crutch and struck the big cop's cell phone, breaking the screen. And again.

The big cop's babbled wrath an animal sound. Rugg thought of Rose, how broken he would find her. His beautiful daughter.

"Walk," he said.

They moved down the hallway. Rugg's mobile vibrated again. At the stairs he instructed them to descend and sit on the bottom step. He waited. When they sat, he slipped his arm inside the crutch handles and slung them to his shoulder. He descended with his free hand on the bannister, his weapon pointed at their backs. The lobby empty, the old man behind the desk. Rugg stopped on the stairs to look at him. He raised the pistol to his lips to signal silence. The old man's eyes wide under the cap brim. Rugg ordered the men to get to their feet and to advance into the middle of the lobby. He told the commander to sit in the chair. The big cop he told to drop to his knees. When Rugg stood behind them, he told the commander to move to the door.

"Follow him on your knees," he said to the big cop.

The commander held the door, while the big cop exited on his knees. Rugg followed. The street without traffic. The night deceptively fresh. They stood without shadows, antipathetic strangers brinked to hell's edge. Their faces white in the neon tubelight.

Rugg surveyed the block. A Buick Verano and an Acura sedan the only vehicles parked before the hotel. "Who drove?" he asked. The commander said he had come alone in the Acura. Rugg told him to set the bundled money and the duct tape on the Buick's hood and to empty the big cop's pockets onto the decklid. The commander removed a wallet, vehicle keys, loose change, and a penknife from the cop's pockets. The keys hung with a button fob. Rugg instructed him to keep the wallet and to swipe the penknife and change off the car. Then he told the commander to unlock the Buick's decklid.

The big cop was ordered off his knees and into the trunk of his own car after Rugg eyed it for weapons. When he balked, Rugg struck him in the groin with a crutch. "Get in or run," he said. The Buick's compartment a tight fit for a big man. After the cop climbed in, Rugg told Magaña to close the decklid and to put the tape and the money on the back seat.

"Check the fuel," he said when they were inside.

The commander started the big cop's Buick. "Full," he reported.

They drove, Rugg in the back seat. The Buick with darkly tinted glass. Rugg slid the mobile from his pocket and powered it off without looking at it. "How far?" he asked.

"One of the neighborhoods."

"What is it called?"

The commander told him. Rugg recognized the name as the one the taxista had given him when they had reconnoitered the private clubs.

"How do you know she is there?"

"I made inquiry."

"Right. After I put money on the table."

Magaña glanced in the rearview. "Believe me when I tell you, Mr. Rugg, your carjacking was not reported. You were found shot, and Tomás sent you to the hospital. I do not offer excuses for him, but he did not know your daughter was gone until he saw her photo."

"Is that his name? Tomás?"

Commander Magaña nodded. "A highway cop must learn to live with these unforgiving men, for his own safety, for the safety of his family. There is no other way. These men transit with a higher power than the law — the power of knowing a cop can be replaced by one who listens better, and he can be replaced by one who is blind, and he by the sightless who is stricken dumb. There are no men riding donkeys here. It is how a highway cop lives."

"She had better be there," Rugg said.

They drove, Rugg watching how the commander's eyes trolled the road, a man in search of a detour around this fix. "Don't be a fool," he warned. "You will be the first to go."

The city center left behind. The street signs with the cardinal point abbreviations routing north of the hotel and away from the airport. Rugg pulled the big cop's pistol from his waist and gripped the sound suppressor to test the lock. When he checked the safety, he found the weapon ready to fire. Rugg knew a man's gun told much about him — his fear and forethought. He toggled the catch and returned the pistol to his waist before he removed from his pocket the commander's compact, finding the safety set. He laid the compact beside him on the seat.

Rugg knew the big cop could not remain inside the Buick when they stopped for Rose. "Do you know where to find them?" he asked.

"Who?"

"The ones who took my daughter."

The commander shook his head. "What end would that bring, Mr. Rugg? If you have your daughter, you have no need to find them. No good will come of it."

"Do you know?"

"They have many houses. Like rats have holes."

"Where?"

"Everywhere."

"Give me one on the highway. What's the town?"

"Mr. Rugg, I am an office cop. I am out of touch with the field. I do not see them. They do not see me."

"Does Tomás know?"

"I don't know what he knows."

"What's his name, the boss?"

"What boss?"

"The gavillero boss who speaks English."

Commander Magaña did not look at Rugg in the mirror. "I know him only by his sobriquet. They call him El Sin."

"El Sin? Why El Sin?"

"Because he is without something, I suppose."

"Without what?"

Magaña shrugged. "I can't say. Pity, maybe?"

Rugg asked what he knew about the man so-called.

"I know only that he is ex-military, that he gets no trouble from traffickers."

The streets narrowed. They drove through a barrio of low-slung dwellings, none stuccoed, their windows dark. Rugg looked for a spot. "Stop here," he said.

"What?"

"Pull over."

They stopped before a vacant lot, the streetlight distant. Scrawled on the lot's wall a graffiti message: Zona Libre de Inmortales. Rugg told Magaña to kill the motor and the lights and to lower the passenger-side window and to remove the keys from the ignition.

"Mr. Rugg ..."

"Shut up. Turn on the dome light and toss the keys out the window."

The commander obeyed.

"Put both hands on the wheel and keep them there. Eyes forward. If I see the hands come off, you'll know it."

He sat with his hands holding the wheel. Rugg pocketed the commander's compact before he descended with the crutches.

The keys lay on the ground near the door. Rugg took them and pressed the fob to lock the Buick's doors. He moved beside the vehicle before he released the trunk's decklid. Inside, the big cop a crumpled shape. Rugg poked him with a crutch. When the cop lifted his head, Rugg reached down and tore the tape off his mouth. "Get out."

The cop squinted in the trunk light. "¡Hijo de la chingada!" his first words. He writhed and rolled to rise from the trunk.

The street tenantless except for dogs. Rugg glanced at the commander seated in the lighted Buick. "Don't move," he warned. When the big cop got to his feet, Rugg closed the decklid. He told the cop to turn around and move away from the vehicle. "Where do I find El Sin?" he asked.

The big cop snickered. "He'll find you, fool."

Rugg jabbed the cop's back with the crutch. "Where?"

"Screw your mother, gringo! Screw your daughter."

The Smith & Wesson Rugg laid on the decklid. He pulled from his waist the cop's machine pistol before he retucked the Smith & Wesson. "Where is he?"

"You won't …"

"Walk."

"What?"

"Walk." Rugg shoved him with the crutch.

"You're dead, gringo. Your whore kid is dead. I'll make sure of it."

When Rugg struck him a second time, the cop walked into the lot. Rugg followed. He turned to check the Buick. The commander watched them.

"Don't stop," he told the big cop.

At the back of the lot a brick wall. When Rugg released the safety on the machine pistol, the big cop stopped. "Wait!"

"Where do I find him?" Rugg asked.

The cop started to turn around.

"Don't look," Rugg said. "Where is he?"

"El Sin doesn't have your kid, gringo."

"I know. Tell me where he is."

"He is not in one place."

"Where do they go from the highway?"

"I can't say."

When Rugg shot the ground at the cop's feet, the pistol quiet. The popping dirt made the big cop jump. "Where?"

"I don't know."

Rugg glanced at the commander.

"Don't shoot," the cop said.

Rugg waited. "Anything else?"

"What?"

"Do you have anything else to say?"

"I don't understand."

"Yes, you do. Turn around."

The big cop faced him. Rugg did not ask the cop why he robbed adolescent girls of their innocence and bragged of the obscenity. He knew the cop would have no answer. "Why did you bring a silencer?" he asked.

"What?"

"This pistol has a silencer. Why did you bring it to the hotel?"

The big cop said the pistol was one he carried in his vehicle.

"This is not police armament," Rugg observed. "Did you come to kill me and make no noise doing it?"

"No."

Rugg watched him in the dim light, how he shrunk. Gone the smug defiance. The big cop not so big backed to a wall.

"You should not have told me," Rugg said.

"What?"

"What you said at the hotel."

"I lied."

"About the old man at the desk? That was not a lie."

"What?"

"You did not lie about harming him. You were clear. That makes it my next best reason."

"What?"

"Your mother heard you, cop."

"What?"

The pistol's discharges a whisper in the loud night. Rugg shot multiple rounds into the big cop until only the wall stood before him. Twenty years since Rugg had shot a man, and he felt the same. Nothing. The firearm seemed an accurate weapon, and he did not check its former owner for survival but turned and aimed the pistol at the Buick. The commander kept his hands on the wheel. Rugg crutched toward him. He unlocked the doors with the fob and he set the crutches inside. "You won't have to share," he said before he got in and gave the keys to the commander.

15

I stand near a tree across the street from the hotel and pretend to wait for a bus. The traffic is thin. Some batos still run with their headlights. One ride sits in front of the hotel. I can't tell if it's an Acura or a high-end Honda. The hotel is dead. I don't see window movements or any comings and goings, but I hear a hum from the hotel light that's hung outside. I check the phone for battery charge, and I make sure the Colt is covered by my shirt. The news that the badass gringo walks on crutches makes me think I can outrun him. That he rides in a Ford Ranger makes me think he's looking for his kid, the gringa. For sure, he picked a dead hotel and not a tourist standout, but he might as well go to the moon to get back his blondie. That girlie joint won't let him inside, and the gorilla in the suit won't let her leave. He's milking batos with that gringa. I'm no judge of daddies — stepdaddies I know about — but I figure the gringo daddy would be better off dead than finding his kid in a whorehouse. There's no going back to yesterday after that news hits. I don't feel sorry for him or for her. It's not my business to care. My business is to wait. I hang near the tree, and after a few buses go by, I move down the block.

There's a tortilla shop opening on the corner, and there's a beer store that's been open all along. Everything looks normal, except for a woman who hits a bato with a brick outside the beer store. The bato is on the ground, and the woman stands over him, serving him a solid beatdown. I guess the brick was handy. The ruckus is big enough that sidewalk busybodies turn into a crowd. I move back to the tree and stare at the dead hotel.

No Ford Ranger pulls in. The hotel door doesn't open. The sedan parked in front is an Acura — not a Honda — one of the luxury models. It's a fancy ride for a crummy hotel, but I know the deal: batos with nice rides park at crummy hotels to be with women who aren't their wives. Perico says so. I'm thinking this hotel might be a good place to boost a ride from a cheating bato, and I'm thinking I'll pass the tip on to Zuky for future jobs, when the Cherokee pulls up beside me and the windows go down. Zuky wears his mask on the top of his head. The mask is painted with horns and grinning teeth, which makes him look like a devil. "Are you awake, dumbass?" he begins. I don't answer because it's an opener, not a question. When he asks if I've seen anything, I tell him I saw a woman hitting a bato with a brick outside the beer store. It gets a laugh from Perico, who sits inside with Niquelado, Tecolote, and Fer, all of them showing hardware. El Sin isn't with them. "Enough jokes, dumbass," Zuky barks. "We'll be on Serdán, watching for him." The Cherokee rips off, and I get out of the way before it does. I don't mention boosting rides from cheaters at the hotel. I leave it for later.

THE VACANT LOT left behind when Commander Magaña spoke. "That's a big problem," he said.

They drove.

"This is his car."

"I know," Rugg said.

They drove.

"How do I know you won't shoot me?"

Rugg told him that if he did nothing foolish, if he delivered Rose to the airport, he would be a rich cop instead of a dead one. "As you said, Commander, our fortunes derive from a specific cause. Greed will keep you alive. Stupidity won't."

They drove.

"Still, it is a problem. He will be seen."

"Drive," Rugg said. He unscrewed the suppressor from the cop's pistol and detached the magazine. He wiped both on his shirt before he rolled down the window and threw one after the other into the street. The commander glimpsed Rugg in the mirror. After clearing the chamber, Rugg threw out the round and wiped the pistol and pitched it. The Smith & Wesson he took from

his lap. He leveled it at the commander. "How much longer?" he asked.

"Not long."

"You will get down and bring her," Rugg explained. "Leave it running."

Commander Magaña said he would speak with the club owner first. "An arrangement must be made."

Rugg told him to do what he had to do. "You're a cop with a two hundred-thousand-peso receivable. Grease the wheels."

The commander nodded.

"If you do not return in ten minutes, I will do the arranging. Then you will be of no use to me."

Bravado his mask. How he would extract Rose on his own without endangering her, he did not know. What he knew was that saving her was but the beginning of hell's retreat.

He lowered the gun and looked behind them. When they turned a corner, Rugg recognized the neighborhood. The Buick's tires ticked on the paving stones. Ahead, the rotating beacons of police cars dazzled the darkness. The two-story house with cops outside. "Stop," he said.

They watched from a distance.

"What is this?"

"I don't know. Something happened."

A Red Cross ambulance sat double-parked, its lightbar flashing, the exhaust smoke white.

They waited. "Drive in front," Rugg instructed. "Ask from the window."

"What?"

"Ask. Don't get down. Tell them you're a cop."

The commander eased the Buick forward.

"First trouble, you're dead." Rugg tucked the weapon under his shirt.

They pulled even with the ambulance before the commander lowered his window. Two Red Cross paramedics sat in the cab. One drank a bottle of orange soda.

"¿Qué pasó?" the commander asked. He pulled a shield from his shirt pocket and showed it.

The medic driver said there had been a ruckus and a pistol-whipping. He said he did not know more.

"Send me one of the officers," the commander ordered.

The medic who drank the soda got down.

Rugg observed a group of girls corralled at the front of the house. They sat on the grass in their party dresses, no shoes. He took in their painted faces one by one. None looked over eighteen.

"Do you see her?" the commander asked, his voice low.

"No."

The municipal cop who approached carried an assault rifle slung across his chest. After the commander identified himself, the cop reported that several armed customers had entered the club and slapped around some girls before they gave the owner a good buffaloing. When the commander asked if any of the girls had been harmed, the cop shook his head. "They're whores. What's to harm?"

The commander nodded.

"But a pair were carried off."

"A pair?"

"Of whores. Takeout for these bad boys." The cop bent to look through the driver's window at Rugg but did not address him. "If you've come to play, Chief, you're too late," he said.

Commander Magaña said he was looking for a particular favorite, a young blondie.

"That's all of them," the cop replied, pointing to the girls corralled in front.

"None inside?"

The municipal cop shook his head. "If you don't see her there, the club in Colonia Morelos has young ones."

The commander thanked him. Rugg surveyed the house. The double doors open. Inside, a polished floor and glass-topped tables set with bottles and beer cans, some toppled. Here his daughter had endured. He watched the girls on the grass. Some held their knees. Others lay with their legs flung out. How teens waited. Several cops stood guard, talking and laughing, their buoyant shadows cast across the huddled girls.

Commander Magaña and the municipal cop shook hands, wishing each other a good night. Rugg watched out the window. When the Buick dropped off the paving stones, he told the commander to drive the neighborhood.

They crisscrossed the streets and alleys, Rugg checking darkened doorways and empty lots. The Buick overtaken by two patrol trucks carrying the party-clad girls in the truck beds.

"Do you think she was taken?" Magaña asked.

"You tell me," Rugg answered. "How recent is your information that my daughter was there?"

"Two days ago. Tomás saw her."

Rugg silent. An hour too late, he thought. The hour it had taken to load a big cop into the trunk of a car, unload him, and walk him to his interrogation and execution. He told the commander to backtrack to the nearest crossroads.

They drove. Rugg took the mobile from his pocket and powered it on. Two missed calls from Sue. A text with the numbers of the wired money.

"Tomás must have told them," the commander volunteered. "He showed off your picture. Of course, we cannot ask him now."

Rugg closed the mobile. "Where would they go?" he asked.

The commander shrugged.

"Don't shrug." Rugg watched his eyes.

"I told you, they have many holes. Where do rats go? Out of sight."

The streets daylit. Rugg saw laborers with bundled lunches and water jugs, some riding bicycles, their lives lived beyond his troubles. Their troubles borne beyond what his life would know. He considered how to proceed, and he weighed the possibility that the gavilleros would ransom his daughter or conspire with law enforcement for abetment in the pursuit of the reward. Then he considered what was most likely: that they would use Rose as bait. Or worse — put her out of reach.

"Where now?" Magaña asked.

Rugg's gaze broke from the street. He thought about the big cop, where he lay. He told the commander to pull over. After the Buick stopped, Rugg handed him the mobile and instructed him to call into the comandancia and report that he would be unavailable for the day due to a personal matter. When the call ended, Rugg told him to drive to the hotel.

16

A Buick Verano with tinted windows pulls up at the hotel and parks beside the Acura. I'm watching for a white Ford Ranger with no plates, so I don't give the Buick a second look until the passenger door opens. Even with a ball cap on his head, there's no mistaking the big gringo. So much for driving a Ranger.

He gets down full length and stands on metal crutches. Sure enough, he's missing a foot. The last time I saw him, he was badassing on both feet, tugging and shoving with tough-guy moves. Now he doesn't look so tough. He looks thin, but he still has the pissed-off face. I watch him crutch to the Acura. Next, I see a well-dressed bato get down from the driver's side of the Buick. He walks to the Acura and gets behind the wheel. Zuky never mentioned a chauffeur, but when I think about it — driving one-footed can't be easy. The gringo climbs into the back seat.

I pull out the phone and call. I don't expect Zuky to answer, and he doesn't. After I hang up, I stay by the tree. My chance to get him on crutches is over for now, and I can already hear Zuky calling me a dumbass. I check the street, expecting to see our Cherokee turn the corner, but it doesn't. The gringo and the bato sit in the car. I wait. This is when El Sin would walk over and shoot. That's what I'm thinking when I see the backup lights come on. Then the Acura is rolling.

THE HOTEL QUIET when they parked beside the commander's Acura. Rugg told Magaña to leave the keys in the ignition. He dropped the duct tape and the bundled money on the front seat and he instructed the commander to bring them. Rugg descended with his weapon concealed, his eyes on Magaña. Inside the Acura he asked for a fuel check.

"Three quarters."

"If there are weapons here, tell me now," he said.

The commander shook his head. "This is my wife's car."

Rugg sat weighted with sleepless hours. His leg throbbed. He knew the big cop's body would be seen from the street. "The money is at the telegraph office," he said. "If you want it, cooperate. Any trouble, I shoot and take my chances."

He checked behind them. No vehicles sat opposite the hotel. Down the street stood a thin youth looking the other way. "Give me his wallet," he said.

Magaña took the big cop's wallet from his pocket and handed it back. The wallet thick with cash. Rugg emptied the leather sleeves of printed cards, reading each. None with handwritten messages or phone numbers. He did not regret breaking the cop's phone, a deed that brought him to search a dead man's wallet for clues. *Check my phone,* the cop had said when he spoke of Rose — an invitation that had unmanned Rugg beyond any foul prospect in his life. He regarded the cop's driver's license, his picture, the toothy grin. Gone to hell's cellar, Rugg hoped. Ablaze upon the igneous premise. He set the wallet on the seat beside him, and he told the commander that an honest cop would get the wallet's money to the big cop's widow.

"Tomás was not married, Mr. Rugg."

"He said his wife is pregnant."

"He lied."

"Is his mother dead?"

"Yes."

Rugg said the news made it easy to give the money to whoever found his daughter. "You must live to find her, Commander."

When he rechecked the street, the thin youth still stood there. Rugg observed how his shirtfront bulged at the waist. The youth wore sneakers.

"Back out and make a U-turn," he said.

The commander started the Acura and reversed. Rugg edged closer to the window. When the Acura came out of the turn, the youth didn't move. He stood with his hand on his waist. "Stop at the tree," Rugg said. He pressed the window's power button as the Acura curbed, and he leveled the pistol at the youth. "¿Qué esperas?" he asked.

The youth dropped his hand from his waist. He stared at Rugg but didn't answer. His face without the years to grow out a mustache. His eyes older than what they had seen. A punk.

"What are you waiting for?" Rugg repeated.

"Nothing."

"Watching the hotel?"

The punk said he was waiting for a bus.

Rugg asked what was under his shirt.

"Nothing."

"Show me nothing." Rugg kept his eyes on him, even as he spoke to Magaña. "Hands on the wheel, Commander."

The punk did not lift his shirt. His left sneaker turned out. The dirt scuffed where he stood.

If not him, Rugg thought, another like him shed of mask in a world that spun smaller until the finders became the found and the found were still sought. He shot the first round near the punk's feet, the dirt spitting, the detonation sharp like a backfire. The commander flinched and swore. When the punk jumped, Rugg glimpsed the pistol, its silver grip.

"Put the gun on the ground," he said.

His stance shifted, the bad foot favored. Eyes cast to the street, beyond where they could see. Then Rugg knew. He aimed the second shot just above his head and into the tree. The commander's knuckles white on the wheel. When the punk reached for his waist, Rugg warned him. "Slowly."

He laid the pistol near the curb. Rugg checked the street. He knew the punk would spot them first, this fortuity wasted should he run. He pointed his weapon at the skinny gut. "Get in or die," he said.

Not all at once did the punk's tough guy expression fade — as if no one before Rugg had so plainly proposed his death. Doubt distrusted.

Rugg watched him limp. "Front seat." After the punk closed the door, Rugg opened his own and took the pistol. He had shut the door when he heard his name called through the window.

"Mr. Rugg. ¡Cuidado!"

Across the street Pedro sat in the Ranger, his Dodgers cap tilted skyward. He had brought the truck from behind the hotel, parking it in the space vacated by the Acura. Rugg gestured for him to scram. "¡Vete, Pedro!" he called. He jerked his arm to convey urgency, but the old man only waved. Rugg told the commander to drive.

They'd reached the next block when he saw the black Cherokee turn off a side street and accelerate toward them, too fast for sane transit. Rugg lowered his weapon. The Cherokee blew past them, its occupants but gray shadows behind the tinted glass. The punk followed their passing before Rugg leaned forward and cuffed him. "Eyes front." When he looked back, he saw the Cherokee stopped in front of the hotel. He hoped the old man had driven away.

"Where?" asked the commander.

"The highway. Don't speed."

Rugg certain they outgunned him beyond a survivable advantage. When he saw no vehicle follow, he told the punk to empty his pockets on the console. Rugg ejected the magazine from the pistol and set it on the seat beside him. The pistol a Colt, its grips engraved with a snake-and-eagle design, the silver handworn by the salted grips of shooters lived before this punk glimpsed the world. Rugg stuck the Colt in his waist. When he checked the rear glass, he did not see the Cherokee.

The punk dropped pocket change on the console.

Rugg cuffed him again. "No phone?"

He pulled a flip phone and set it on the console.

Rugg took the phone and opened it. He found one number called, no connection minutes logged. He read the dial time and checked his watch. The Cherokee had been nearby. Rugg put the phone in the seat pocket in front of him. "Where's my wallet?" he asked.

The punk said he didn't know about a wallet.

Rugg leaned forward and cuffed him harder than the time before. "You took it and you winked. Don't you remember?"

"I don't know nothing," he said.

Rugg sat back, his next step weighed. This punk sent to surveille him by the men who had taken her. Ransom not their plan. Kill him, their plan.

They drove out of the city. At the highway Rugg looked behind them before he told the commander to turn north. He poked the punk in the arm with the Smith & Wesson. "You're going to help me," he said.

When the punk started to turn, Rugg cuffed him and told him not to look back. "You're taking me to my daughter."

He stared ahead. "You are confused, gringo."

Rugg said he was a gringo but not a confused one. "Who did you call?"

The punk shrugged. His seat belt unbuckled. Rugg reached over the punk's head and grabbed the metal tongue from the pillar loop and slung the sash across his neck. He pulled and held it against the seatback, watching the punk try to lift the belt off his throat. "Who did you call?"

The punk used both hands.

"Who?"

When he didn't answer, Rugg tightened the belt. "Who?"

"Zuky?"

"Is that a name?"

He nodded.

"What about El Sin. Is he your boss?"

The punk unable to wedge his thumbs under the belt.

"Is he? Move your head."

He nodded.

"Does he have my daughter?" Rugg twisted out any slack. "Does he?"

No answer. His neck under the headrest. When Rugg heard him gurgle, he released the belt.

The punk pitched forward. He coughed and grabbed his throat. "Qué poca madre," he spat. A blood line marked his neck where the belt had cut.

The commander stared ahead. Rugg silent, the Smith & Wesson riding one knee. From his shirt pocket he removed the photocopy with Rose's picture. He unfolded it and held it out for the punk to see. "This is my daughter. Does he have her?"

He looked. He said he did not remember any gringas.

Rugg eyed him, the bony toughness. Not much older than Rose, but years lived beyond hers. "Where did they take her?"

"I don't know nothing," he repeated.

"You don't know, or you don't want to say?"

"I don't know nothing."

They drove. Rugg checked behind them before he took the big cop's wallet and laid it on the console where the punk could see the cash. "Help me out," he said. "Where is she?"

The punk looked and then looked away. He touched his throat. The commander said the punk was a good-for-nothing street punk.

Rugg asked if his daughter was in or out of the city. When no reply came, he reached for the seat belt. The punk lifted his hand. He said that knowing nothing was knowing that the gringa worked as a whore in a girlie place, and that was all he knew and no more.

Rose's picture folded and returned to Rugg's pocket. "Old news," he told the youth. "Your bosses took her."

Rugg watched him, how he showed no surprise. A clueless punk or one beyond clever.

"The girlie joint is all I know," he said.

The commander called him a liar. Rugg certain that any truth spoken by this youth sounded no truer than if he lied.

They drove. The desert on either side without range fence, the scrub thick. Rugg checked behind them. The highway not a place to further this interrogation, he decided.

At kilometer signpost thirty-one he told Magaña to slow the Acura. He took the punk's phone from the seat pocket and checked the signal bars before he instructed the commander to take the first brecha that broke from the highway.

The brecha narrow and rutted. The sedan lifted dust. "Will he answer when I call?" he asked the punk.

"What?"

"Your boss. Will he answer when I call from your phone?"

"I don't know nothing."

Rugg read the number. "Don't know? OK. Here's something you should know — the man who drives us is a cop."

The punk said nothing. When the scrub opened into an arroyo fan-out wide enough for a turnaround, Rugg told the commander to stop and back up.

"If your boss answers, I will tell him you are with a Federal Police commander, and I will tell him the names you gave us. This Zuky and El Sin."

The punk almost turned. "You lie, gringo."

Rugg said that lies were truths until proven otherwise. "I will tell him where to find you on this brecha," he added. "You can take your chances with that, or you can help me."

He shrugged. "I don't know where she is. I'm a lookout."

"A lookout with a pistol," Rugg corrected.

The punk said nothing. Rugg pulled the Colt and reloaded the magazine before he snugged it under his belt. "I saw you reach. The magazine is full."

The punk said nothing.

Magaña told the punk he was a stupid, good-for-nothing lookout who couldn't outrun a lamppost or shoot one.

The punk shrugged again. Call whoever whenever, he said, it was all the same to him.

Rugg pressed the phone's Call button. When no one answered, he waited before he called again, letting it ring. And again. The punk stared at the desert. Rugg closed the phone and dropped it on the seat. He checked his watch and sat with the near certainty that this punk who had fallen from the sky to advert him was a stroke of luck come hours too late to save Rose from where she had been. So what was the advantage now? Hold him and wait for a callback that might not come? Broker a trade with men who wanted him dead? Squeeze this punk until the near certainty became a certainty or until he gave up value? And then what? And meanwhile, the three of them riding in an Acura?

Rugg saw himself as he sat one-footed, holding at gunpoint a dirty cop and a shifty punk, and how their cooperation hinged on his divided advertence and close-quarter marksmanship — a precarious formula should he get tired or careless. Meanwhile the clock ticking. Gavilleros and a dead cop on his heels. The punk certain to bolt at the earliest slipup. Better to lose him here for what he might give up than to lose him later for nothing.

He told the commander to lower the passenger windows, turn off the ignition, and put the keys on the console. Rugg took them and pocketed the cop's wallet before he opened the door and descended on his crutches into the bright morning. "Keep your hands on the wheel, Commander." He ordered the punk to get out and move away from the Acura.

Rugg watched him limp. The Smith & Wesson he held at the crutch handle.

The punk stopped and looked at him.

"Final offer, cabroncito," Rugg said. "Get back in the car and take us to your houses. Highway and city. One by one. Not made-up places. I want to see proof. You do that, no harm."

The punk spat. "I don't drive. Only ride."

"With your eyes open you ride."

"I don't know nothing," he repeated.

"Sure?"

"I said I don't know …"

"OK. You know the drill. Run."

The punk didn't move. He looked at the Colt braced in Rugg's waist.

"Run."

He stood.

"I'm out of time," Rugg said.

The punk told Rugg that he wore them too large to run.

"Too large?"

He nodded. Swagger in his uneven stance.

"We'll see."

With the first shot Rugg dropped him, the round splitting the sneaker of his good foot. He suspected the punk had sold himself short on the prospect of gunfire.

"¡Pinche gringo, puta madre!" he swore.

Rugg crutched to where he cursed and kicked the dirt. Blood leaked from his sneaker. He told the punk that if he wore them large enough not to run, he should wear them large enough to shut up. Rugg pointed the pistol at the punk's face. "Where's my daughter?"

"¡No sé, chingado — no sé!" he answered.

"Know nothing again?"

"¡No sé!"

"OK." In Rugg's experience, the prospect of a second bullet prompted most gunshot men to forgo the risk of falsehood if the truth seemed more likely to spare them.

As for boys, he assumed the same likelihood, though this was the first boy Rugg had shot. He took the big cop's wallet from his pocket and dropped it on the ground. The punk kicked and hollered. Rugg told him the money in the wallet was for a doctor, should he reach one. Then he ascended the Acura.

The commander said, "You should finish him."

Rugg watched the punk from his window. "Like your cop?"

"Like a snake. Before he grows fangs."

The punk writhed on his side, the desert on him.

"Drive," Rugg said.

They left the fan-out and retook the highway. He told the commander to double back to the city, and then he asked for the highway emergency toll number. Rugg took the punk's flip phone and dialed. He told the operator he had witnessed a shooting at kilometer 31 off the northbound lanes, approximately one hundred meters east of the asphalt. "The suspect is armed and dangerous," he added before he hung up.

They drove in silence. Rugg pulled the Colt pistol and sighted it before he put it in the front-seat pocket. Had he squeezed the punk too soon, he asked himself. Would patience have rendered him pliable and so guarantee that he knew no more than he said?

Screw patience. No time for it.

The punk's loyalty to his bosses lay beyond any promise of remuneration or redemption. His shrug, his wink, his defiance were proven defenses: how the godforsaken showed their allegiance to the murderous, and, in turn, lived to wink and shrug again, to defy what the murdered had not. One prospect certain: the punk had been given a better chance than he to crawl out of the desert.

"Obey the speed limit," Rugg said and nothing else. The commander's hands on the wheel what he watched. Gone the fatigue. No amount of sleep would rest what was left of him until he found her. The pain in his leg a tonic to sooth the gaping hole she had left.

17

The badass comes at me like an Apache. I don't expect to see a gun, but this gringo is full of lies and tricks. He tries to buy me with wallet cash and he tries to bluff me with his driver — who doesn't look like a cop but more like a bato who owns an Acura. Then there's the seat belt, which he uses to choke me. It's a first, and worse than I imagined. He's smoked about all my know-nothings, but I've got nothing to share about his kid, except where she works. He calls that old news, which means he knows more than I do. What I know is that Zuky won't pick up his cell, no matter how many times someone calls. Dialing God — that's what Zuky calls it — no answer.

When the gringo tells me to get down from the Acura, I figure he's come to where he can't stand me, which is why he drove to the desert. He knows I was supposed to shoot him at the hotel. There's no backing out of that, not after he saw me reach for the Colt. He wants me to think I can spring myself by giving up our crash houses, but I don't buy it. The gringo will say anything to get his kid. Then he tells me to run, which is a joke because neither of us can run. I figure him for a lousy shot, aiming from a crutch handle, but he hits me first try. I don't hear the pop until the dirt spits up. The desert flips sideways, but it's really me flipped on my side with my foot caught on fire and my ears filled with hollering. Blood squirts from the hole in my sneaker. Then the badass stands over me jawing. When he aims at my face and asks about his daughter, I give him another know-nothing. There's a chance it's one know-nothing too many — my last know-nothing — but I can't give up what I don't know. Instead of shooting me, he drops something on the ground and he crutches his badass back to the Acura. I hear the motor start.

They leave me in the dust rollout, and I save my curses because they'd be wasted. When I sit up, my head gets dizzy, and I press my hands to the ground to stop the wobble. I look at my shoe. It's the color of my blood and still leaking. I see the hole where the bullet went in, but I don't see one where it went out, and I don't know if one hole is better than two, but my foot already feels too big for the shoe. I look across the clearing. It's a good shade-less spot for bad luck to get worse. I'm hot and sweated and thirsted, and the sun is so bright the dirt looks white. When I look behind me, I see what the gringo dropped. It's the wallet — the one he put on the console — still thick with cash, which is another badass joke. I've lifted lots of wallets without keeping any, and here's one I didn't lift that comes from the bato who shot me. I'm not in a mind to make sense of it.

I try to stand on my crooked foot, which isn't practiced for one-legged standing. The first try, I fall. Second try, the same. I wait and nerve up, holding to the hot dirt. My sneaker feels like it's full of sand. On the third try I stay up, but that sets off a hammer pounding a big nail into the bullet hole. I clamp my jaw to bite off a cry and tell myself to wear 'em. When I look down, the dirt is dark where blood drips from the shoe. I hop two steps and wait, daring my shot foot to touch the ground for balance. Then I hop again and wait. It's hard work, and I don't get far before the hammering in my foot reaches my head. The wallet I leave behind. Losing cash is better than losing blood, and I couldn't pick it up anyway. Hopping is what I do. Hop and stop.

How far we drove from the highway is hard to remember. I listen for traffic noise but don't hear any. A buzz starts up in my ears, which doesn't help. I'm still in the arroyo when I see dust rise from a vehicle coming fast down the brecha. I hope it's our crew — not the gringo — and then I see the flashing lights and the shapes of men with rifles standing in a pickup. The truck stops, and the first cop who comes knocks me to the ground with his rifle butt. He orders me to stay down, which I do.

THEY STOPPED AT A convenience store where Rugg made the commander park in the space nearest the entrance. Through the plate-glass window he watched the cashier. No one else moved inside the store. He told the commander to get down and buy water with his own money. "If I see you open your mouth, I will shoot you through the glass." Then Rugg told him to hand over the keys.

The commander descended and returned with the bottled water. Rugg surveyed the perimeter before he unlocked the Acura and told Magaña to drive from the store. On a side street they stopped and drank the water.

"Who runs the city police?" Rugg asked.

Magaña said the municipal captain was responsible for the patrol units.

Rugg maximized the volume on his mobile before he handed it to the commander. "Call him. Ask for help."

He took the phone. "What do you want me to say? It would not be wise to tell too much."

"Tell him you lost a girl last night. Tell him where. Tell him you went to see her, that his patrolmen were there, that they told you she was taken by some customers.

Ask him if she is in custody." Rugg advised him not to elaborate beyond the essential or the call would be his last.

The commander dialed and identified himself. After a wait, he was put through to the municipal captain. Magaña detailed the hour and the location of the girl's disappearance. "She is a young blonde," he added. "Very young. A minor." The captain chuckled. He asked if the girl was his candy or the candy of another.

"A friend's," Magaña replied. "A friend who is concerned."

Rugg listened to the captain say he knew nothing. "Let me check with the barandilla sergeant," he said. Then he put the call on hold.

They waited. Magaña drank water. Rugg found himself forced to contemplate another option, one that made him sick to consider. "Morgue," he said to the commander. "Ask if he knows of any girls sent there."

When the captain's voice came on the line, it was to report that no minors were in custody. Magaña said the news was bad tidings of a sort, and then he asked the captain as a personal favor to check with the morgue for any arrival who fit the description. "I would call myself, but an inquiry from a federal agent might bring undue attention."

"This sounds like candy in trouble," the captain observed.

Magaña said the young blonde was in enough trouble that it was not a joke. "Please call me," he said before he hung up.

Rugg checked his watch. He told the commander to start the Acura and retake the nearest avenue that crossed the city.

"I told you the captain would help," Magaña said.

Rugg replied that ascertaining a girl's death was a sorry service if a favor had to be promised. He asked the captain's name.

"Why do you want to know his name?"

"Should I recognize his voice in hell, I will have a name," Rugg said.

They drove.

"Do not take his girlie talk seriously, Mr. Rugg. It is how men speak, even the good ones."

Rugg said he took nothing seriously beyond the recovery of his daughter. He said all men, including himself, were pigs, and, as such, they remained blind to their true nature.

The commander said nothing. They crisscrossed the city, marking time. When Rugg's phone rang, he read the number before he handed the cell to the commander. He listened to the municipal captain tell Magaña that the morgue had received several bodies that day and the day before, none girls.

Magaña thanked him. "We are pending," he added. After he ended the call, he looked at Rugg in the rearview. "That is much relief," he said.

Rugg remained silent. He lifted his shot leg and rested it on his knee. The phantom foot felt, the stump swollen and throbbing. Blood seeped through the folded pantleg, darkening the crease. The wound not elevated since he had left the hotel the night before — what seemed to him a distant past, one that had not preceded the present.

"Now where?" the commander asked.

The next move not one to be pondered at a standstill, Rugg told himself. Anywhere the same as nowhere until he found her. "Just drive," he said. "Drive. Don't talk."

He knew he was flying blind. What had gotten him this far — his years of navigating the stormed and nighted skies above a black planet — had finally proved fallible. Gone the straight line of how to proceed. His instinct to see beyond the unseen cast in doubt, the path ahead unlit. His plight a dark free fall.

He looked to the street. When he saw a Pemex station with multiple islands, he told the commander to turn in and fuel. Rugg pulled cash from his pocket and tossed it on the front seat. "Fill and pay. No small talk." He pushed the bundled money and duct tape to the floor and lowered the window on the pump side.

They fueled. Rugg watched the commander. He observed the vehicles parked at the other islands. All streets with eyes, he knew. The circuitous route of the last hours one not without chance encounters. He checked his phone and saw missed calls from Sue. Her help a life buoy thrown to a drowned man.

He recalled what the big cop had said about the gavillero boss — *He will find you, fool* — this El Sin, so named for his lack of something. Rugg thought the sobriquet better described himself than the man who had left him without daughter and limb. What madness did these fiends follow if not in a name? The name for nothing.

He will find you, fool.

From the seat pocket he removed the punk's flip phone and opened it. On the screen the last number called, the one he had made to the highway emergency service to report an armed and dangerous suspect. A mere suspect now, Rugg reflected. The uncertainty of how far ignorance could be feigned in the face of death the single reason he had not killed the punk but had let him live to save himself. Or not. The wallet left behind should the cops find him; the cops called should they be looking for a cop killer. Payback for Rose.

Rugg scrolled to the number called by the punk outside the hotel. He pressed the Call button and listened. Then he closed the phone, reopened it, and called the number again. He waited before he closed it and dropped it on the seat.

Magaña paid the Pemex dispatcher. Inside the car he told Rugg he needed to use the restroom.

"Piss in your pants," Rugg replied. He instructed him to drive to the hotel.

They drove. Rugg dropped the magazine from the Smith & Wesson and reloaded the rounds shot at the punk, taking them from the stripper clip taped to his leg. He removed the commander's compact from his pants pocket and set it in the grip well on the Acura's passenger door, at hand as a close-quarters weapon. He pressed Magaña to explain why he and the big cop had come to the hotel at an hour when most men slept — was it to rob and kill him? The commander protested. He said he could not speak for Tomás, that he had come solely to negotiate a price for his assistance to advance the recovery of the girl. Rugg called him a liar. He pushed the gun barrel into the commander's ear and flicked off the safety. "Tell the truth?" The commander said there was no other truth to tell but the one he told. Rugg returned the gun to his lap. How this might end, he feared. Lies and truth the same as his search, a circle taking him nowhere and then to where he began. He sat silent, eyeing the streets, his gaze gone to a world where he would see her out the window, where men found their daughters as they had lost them, without reason and because all paths crossed. "Keep your hands on the wheel," he told Magaña. "It's my daughter who is buying your life. I am only paying."

At the hotel they circled the block before they stopped across the street. The big cop's Buick still parked in front, the Hotel San Carlos not the same. Plywood covered the street window. Glass shards littered the asphalt. The hotel stucco cratered by bullet strikes, the entrance barricaded with yellow police tape. "What in the fornication happened?" the commander asked. Rugg looked for the Ford Ranger but did not see it. "Nothing good," he answered, knowing the cascade of his own misfortune had finally fallen on those he had chosen from among all the strangers to be spared, and so he had brought these reckless gavilleros here to wreak havoc in the pursuit of him. When he dialed the hotel desk phone, no one answered. He told the commander to drive to the back of the hotel.

The lot empty, the trash bins full. Rugg instructed Magaña to park the Acura facing the street. He knew they could arrive in a vehicle he would not recognize.

"It is odd that no one has noticed Tomás's car," Magaña observed.

Rugg offered no reply. When the commander said Tomás's partner would be calling the shift sergeant to ask for him, Rugg answered that the shift sergeant would have news soon enough.

He checked his watch before he retook the punk's flip phone and called the gavillero's number again. And again. Between calls his gaze took in the street.

18

I lie in a bed in a room with batos who lie in other beds. My shirt and pants are gone, and I'm naked under the sheet. I see my feet. The crooked one is dirty. The shot one is bandaged up to the toes, and the bandage is red where the blood leaks. The fire inside my shot foot makes me want to cry like a girl, but I don't.

There are no windows in the room. A cop stands at the door. In the next bed there's an old bato wearing a head bandage. His eyes are closed, but his mouth is open with no sound coming from it. He looks dead. I wonder if the cop at the door is guarding me or another patient. He's got a strapped pistol, but his face doesn't have the badass look of someone who shoots batos in a hospital. El Sin has the look. So does XL. Zuky tries to have it. When a nurse comes to the room, I ask her for water. She tells me I'm getting water from the needle in my arm that connects to *a dripping bottle. I tell her my arm is fine, but the rest of me thirsts. I also tell her my foot feels on fire. She doesn't look sorry to hear it. "Talk to the doctor," she says. When I ask about going to the bathroom, she points to a plastic jug hooked on the bed. The jug isn't empty, which means I used it and don't remember, or another bato used it.*

The doctor who comes is a shorty with a mustache that looks drawn with a pencil. He calls himself Dr. Sanchez and he asks how I feel. I give him my low opinion, and this makes him nod. He calls me a lucky boy because he didn't have to cut off my foot. To lose a foot so young would have been a tragedy, he says, and then he tells me that I will walk again but with a limp. He's polite for a doctor talking to the likes of me. He puts on a pair of gloves and unwinds the bandage, and I see the hole the badass gringo shot in my foot. It looks small, considering how much blood leaked out. When the doctor pushes on the hole with his finger, I yelp. I can't help it. "Bueno," he says. "No hay purulencia." He smiles, so I figure that must be good. He says the shoe saved me from more bleeding because it pressed on the hole. He also says I'm lucky the police found me when they did, which is not how I see it. When I ask if he can give me something to cool the fire, he shakes his head and says that due to the unfortunate circumstances that brought me, the police don't want me sedated until I'm questioned. Dr.

Sanchez says he is sorry. He says he does not want to judge me. I ask him if that means he can't give me anything for the fire. He nods and asks what happened to my crooked foot. I tell him, and he says the streets are a dangerous place. I take it as good advice given late. When he asks if I have family, I tell him my parents are dead, which is half true. I don't mention my aunt because I don't want the cops knowing. He starts to talk about something called the Program of Attention to Adolescents at Risk, but he loses me quick. I ask if I can get some water. He nods and says he hopes to see me soon.

The nurse comes to bandage my foot. She pours me a glass of water from a metal pitcher. The water is warm, but I don't complain. I look at the cop by the door. He watches me. His face says I might do something dangerous with a water glass. Gone is the mystery of who's under guard. No one else gets his attention. I feel special, but not in a good way. Only serious crimes get a hospital guard, which is a puzzlement that keeps my thoughts off the fire and gets me thinking about how to get out of the room and past a cop and out of the hospital and into the street with no clothes and limping on a shot foot plus a crooked one. Thinking about it makes me feel worse.

Later two batos come to the room to add to my trouble. One is a ministerial cop. I know the uniform. The other is street-dressed *and wears glasses. After they enter, the guard leaves the room and shuts the door. They come to my bed, and the ministerial asks straight out for my name. I give him a made-up one, and then he asks how I can prove the name. I tell him I can't prove anything, except that I'm in the hospital. The civilian asks me how I got shot in the foot. "By accident," I answer. When he asks for details, I tell him I don't remember. He points to my neck. "How did you get cut?" he asks. "Shaving," I say. The ministerial shakes his head and calls me the son-of-a-smartass liar. I tell him that's his opinion, and he tells me there have been many highway assaults near where I was found. I wait for him to circle back to my shot foot. Instead, he pulls a wallet from his pocket and asks if it's mine. It's the wallet the gringo left after he shot me, the one thick with cash. Now it's empty. I tell the cop I don't own a wallet. He opens it and pulls out a card. When he shows it to me, I see it's a driver's license. He tells me to look at the picture. I look, but not for long, because I don't want to show that I recognize the bato in the picture. He's the big highway cop — the one Cachoro calls Tomás, who patrols the state line. I saw him with a whore in the girlie joint, and I saw him when we stopped in front of the headless Cali. I wonder how a cop lets his wallet get away and how a gringo ends up with it.*

The ministerial eyes me close when he asks if I've ever seen the bato in the picture. I shake my head. The civilian smiles.

The ministerial puts the license in the wallet and the wallet in his pocket, and then he asks me to explain how the wallet was found by the police in the same place where they found me. I say I don't know. "Ask the man in the picture," I say. The ministerial tells me that the man in the picture can't be asked because he was shot dead and robbed of his wallet. He says the man was a Federal Police officer, which makes the crime no ordinary one. I listen, but I don't look at him because I'm still putting it together. Dead cop. Stolen wallet. Badass gringo. I tell him I know nothing about nothing.

The ministerial calls me a liar who's going straight to the filthy fornication of a fornicating prison. He grabs my shot foot and presses his thumb on the bandage where the blood leaks. I screech in a way that's pathetic. I jerk and twist and try to free my foot, but he's got a good grip, and his thumb finds the bullet hole. The pain is worse than getting shot. Hammer and nails don't describe it. He presses his thumb deeper into the hole, and he tells me to confess the truth about the wallet and the cop. I kick at him with my crooked foot, but I can't hit him. He twists his thumb. I curse and cry. The room goes blurry. When I can't wear 'em any longer, I tell him I know about the wallet. He lets go and says, "Talk, rat."

From the next bed the old bato suddenly speaks up. He looks dead, but he isn't. He tells the ministerial that I'm a kid, and that torture is against the law and so is police abuse. The ministerial tells him to shut up and worry about himself. The old bato says he has heard enough prepotent and shameless cops to identify one when he speaks, and all the same and be that as it may, where have all the good cops gone? When the ministerial threatens to arrest him, the old bato goes quiet. I can't see his face, but I like his spark, considering he looks dead.

"Talk, rat," the ministerial says again, and I cough up the soup, telling him how I'm lifted off the street by a crazy one-footed gringo who is looking for his daughter, and how the crazy gringo thinks I know where to find her, which I don't, and after the lifting, he and another bato, who is his driver, take me to the desert in an Acura, and the gringo already has the wallet in the car, and he offers me the money inside the wallet if I give up his daughter, and when I tell him I know nothing, he gets mad and makes me get out, and then he shoots me and he throws down the wallet before he and the bato drive off, which is why I don't know how the wallet got stolen, but the gringo knows, and maybe he shot the cop and maybe he lifted the wallet and maybe he left it with me so it looks like I did the job. After I swear on my dead mother's memory that what I speak is the truth, the ministerial and civilian look at each other, and the ministerial pulls his pistol and cracks my toes with

the butt. I screech and shrink. "Stop lying," he tells me. The old bato comes alive and calls him a dog. The ministerial tells him to shut up, and then he tells me that a one-footed gringo or a gringo of any flavor wouldn't leave a street rat in the desert with a wallet full of cash. "Do I look like a fool?" he asks, and before I answer, he taps the butt of his pistol on my privates. I shake my head. If he hits me there, I know I won't wear 'em — I'll cry like a girl — so I tell him I saw the dead cop once in a girlie joint, and then I tell him that was my only lie. He makes me say it again — that I know the cop on the license — and he looks hard at me before he holsters the pistol. He says that will be enough until he gets me out of the hospital. He promises to see me soon. The civilian doesn't say anything.

After they leave, the guard moves inside the room again. The bandage on my foot is mostly red. I wonder if the doctor will give me something to ice the fire — now that the cop questioning is over — but the doctor doesn't come, and the nurse says she can give me only water. When she leaves, the guard moves into the hall. I see his shadow outside the door. Later in the dark, I hear the old bato say something about a gringo with one foot. He talks like he's dreaming, so I ignore him. I know I'm not sleeping.

THE RINGTONE ON THE punk's flip phone set to a rooster crow. Rugg read the number before he opened the phone and listened without answering.

"You were smart to keep it," the caller said. "Where did you leave him?"

The graveled voice of the boss not heard since he had ordered Rugg's death on the highway.

"You son-of-a-bitch. Where's my daughter?"

Silence. The call empty of background noise. A parked vehicle, Rugg guessed.

"The girl is safe."

"She'd better be. Put her on."

"No."

Rugg tapped the commander's shoulder with the pistol muzzle. When the commander turned, Rugg gestured for him to move the Acura from the hotel lot.

"Put her on."

"No. Come if you want her. Bring whatever you are paying the cop."

Out the window Rugg looked for them, the likely direction of an ambush. After the Acura retook the street,

he checked to see if they were followed. "If you don't put her on, you don't have her," he said.

"She is not at hand, but I have her. If you are saying you do not want to come, just say it, and we are done. You can pay the cop."

Rugg knew how little he had to offer for the sound of her voice. When the commander asked where he should drive, Rugg pressed the flip phone to his shirt. "Drive!"

He checked his watch. The telegraph office closed in an hour.

"Goodbye gringo," the boss said.

"No, wait! Bring her to the phone and I will tell you where to find the boy, your lookout. How's that?"

"The boy can wait."

"You asked where I left him."

"I asked only to save time."

"I left him alive."

"Alive or dead, it is the same."

Rugg heard amusement in the graveled voice.

"How do I know you have her?"

"I would not return your calls, gringo. I would find you and shoot you."

"You tried that."

"Yes, but I did not have her then. Now I am calling."

"That's not much of a guarantee."

"It is not, but it is what I can give you," the boss said. "A man's word is worth nothing. You know that. Not yours, not mine."

"My word is good," Rugg said.

"So you say, but those are words too. Your word will not get your daughter back. Your money might. There is no other way for you. Here is where you stand, my friend. If you do not come, I will sell her a second time. Then you will be obliged to live long enough to find the man who bought her, and she will be obliged to live long enough to be found, unless she is sold again, which means both of you must live long enough to find each other. This is what you gringos call a narrow window of opportunity, right?"

"You son-of-a-bitch."

Silence.

"Hello?" Rugg said.

"'Son-of-a-whoremother,' we say. Whores are the unsacred mothers of Mexico — we would be less without them. Gringas are just bitches — you would be better without them."

"Put her on."

"I told you."

"Maybe you sold her already."

"Maybe I did. Maybe you will come for nothing. Maybe you will die."

"You're the one who's going to die if you don't give me my daughter."

"Maybe. But I do not need your money as much as you need your daughter. You must come to me."

"Maybe I'll bring the cops," Rugg countered.

The boss said cops were not good for saving the innocent or the helpless. He said they were good for saving themselves and for saving the highest bidder. "And you are not the highest bidder."

"But I'm the one with the cop driving."

"You are. One cop. And you have permission to bring him. No harm will come to him. Tomás knows his employment with you will soon end."

Rugg recognized the dead cop's name. "His employment ended," he said. "The car trunk was too small for him."

News that seemed to sink in. A pause before the gavillero spoke. "For a big cop, that is a problem."

"Not a problem anymore," Rugg said. "Now his boss drives. Commander Magaña."

At the mention of his name, the commander glanced in the rearview. Rugg seized on the gavillero's silence, sensing an opportunity to narrow the man's advantage. "The commander does not care about Tomás. He cares about staying alive. If you hand over my daughter and let him keep some of the money, you will get another fish in your pocket. A big fish, bigger than Tomás. A grateful Federal Police commander."

The boss laughed. "You have balls, gringo. Maybe too many. Does Magaña know this?"

"What do you think?"

"I think I can make that deal without you."

"And I think you would have if you could have. Buy a commander with another man's money, leave him indebted — that's not a deal you can make without me."

New sounds rose from the caller's end. The buffeting of window wind, the close voices of men. Moving, Rugg thought.

"I knew you were a gringo who could run. I did not know you would run this far."

Rugg said he was not done. "I want my daughter."

"Then you know what to do."

When Rugg asked for the location, the boss gave the name of a highway town, a street behind the church, a white house with a gate. Rugg remembered the town as one that he and Pedro had visited in the first days of the search for his truck.

"Why not the highway?" Rugg asked.

"Do you want your daughter brought in the trunk of a car? She is small."

Rugg said his girl had better be where he said she was with no harm come to her. "I want safe passage to the airport."

"Your driver is a cop who commands other cops. That is your safe passage."

In the background Rugg heard ranchera music and a radio voice giving the hour.

"Where did you leave him?" the boss asked.

"What?"

"My lookout. Where is he?"

"You said he can wait."

"I said I was saving time. Perhaps you can shoot him for me."

Rugg told him the boy had been left in the desert. "When I have my daughter, you can have the kilometer post."

"I am more interested in the Colt pistol. Did you keep it?"

"That's for you to find out."

He laughed. "You have been a busy gringo."

"Like I said, I'm not done. In two hours I will bring the money. Have her there." Rugg closed the phone.

He took a breath. Her face before him. How he had seen her many times and not since. *Hell yes. Something.*

He told the commander to drive to the telegraph office.

Magaña looked at him in the mirror. "Is there news?"

"Maybe."

The commander said he had heard his name spoken.

"I told him you were assisting."

"Told who?"

"The caller. Now drive."

They drove. Rugg waited for the commander to ask how the caller had come to dial the punk's flip phone, but he did not ask. A question weighed in silence, if weighed at all.

"Be satisfied you are closer to your money," Rugg said.

Outside the telegraph office, Rugg took the Acura keys. He pocketed the compact pistol and he ordered the commander to get down and stay close. "Don't die for it now."

The commander said he was not such a fool. On the sidewalk they passed a discarded plastic bag. Rugg told the commander to put it in his pocket.

No customers inside the office. Two transaction windows open. Rugg picked the woman. The commander stood to one side while he showed her the phone text with the confirmation numbers for the wired money. The teller wrote the numbers on a form and typed them into a terminal before she asked for Rugg's identification. He handed her the laminated replica of his pilot's license.

She examined it and she examined Rugg. "¿Es usted, señor?" she asked. Rugg nodded. When she stated that he didn't resemble the man in the picture, Rugg showed her the crutches. "Un accidente," he added. She asked if he had another identification. Rugg shook his head.

"Un momento," the woman said before she left.

He checked his watch. "Don't move," he told the commander. He saw the teller retreat to the back of the room, where she spoke to a man behind a desk. She showed him Rugg's license. The man rose and came to the window with the license. He told Rugg that due to the amounts of the transfers, the telegraph company required a recipient to present two forms of identification. Rugg said he had one. The clerk apologized for the inconvenience, but such was the policy of Telégrafos de México. Rugg remembered what the old man had said when the teller had questioned his credentials: "Do I look like Juárez on a horse?" He told the clerk that two days earlier he had accompanied a recipient to this office where an equally large sum had been paid out after a single identification was shown. The clerk shrugged. He said it shouldn't have been so, that each supervisor applied his own criteria. Rugg said that didn't sound like policy. The clerk apologized again. When Rugg asked to speak to the supervisor, the clerk said he was the supervisor and fully at the gentleman's service. Rugg considered giving him a brief outline of his predicament, but the clerk's face said empathy amounted to a bureaucratic demerit. Instead, Rugg avowed, "I need it now." The clerk offered his regrets before he returned the license under the transaction window. Rugg did not take it. He pointed to Magaña. He told the clerk that an officer of the law could vouch for him.

"Show him your ID, Commander."

Magaña pulled his shield and held it to the glass. He said he was a federal agent who could affirm the man's identity. He told the clerk that if an additional reference was needed, he should call the Federal Police comandancia. He gave the name and the phone number of the 1st Sergeant.

The clerk looked at the police shield. "Un momento," he said. Then he spoke to the teller.

She returned with the bundled cash, which she counted without breaking the currency straps. Rugg counted to himself. After he signed the receipt, she pushed the cash under the window. Rugg told the commander to put the bundles in the plastic bag he had pocketed. The clerk watched from his desk.

Rugg exited last. On the street he told the commander that should he run with the money or try anything stupid, the first shot would split his back and the second would end his misery. When the commander replied that, if not for him, there would be no money, Rugg said, "Don't play the hero. You just helped yourself."

19

A hospital isn't the place to be if you can't get up and leave. I wonder if Zuky knows I'm here. I wonder if he thinks I ditched the job. Whatever he thinks, my name will have dumbass painted front and back. He'll tell El Sin, and then what, I don't know. Consequences have always been a distant reckoning for me, but lying in a hospital with two bad feet and a fake wrap for killing a cop gets me to reckoning straightaway. Jail or dead is where I see my road forking. I know El Sin's business. El Sin knows cops. Now the cops know me. That seems like a circle — a circle that leads to a fork. Maybe El Sin will bring a crew — what he did for XL at the morgue — except it won't be to rescue me but to put me in the morgue. Or he'll send Güero del Café to clean up the mess. Or maybe I'm nobody enough to bother with, and he'll leave me to the cops. From where I lie, a dead end and an end not dead look the same, like my feet — neither works, but for different reasons.

The fire and the hammer follow me into the next day. A nurse comes and pulls the needle out of my arm, and she puts tape on the hole. Some batos in our room get visitors who bring them food. When I see two pelados come in looking stiff and unfriendly, I think they're civilians of the legal type, bringing me new trouble. But they walk past my bed and stop where the old man lies, not so dead. They speak in low voices, leaning over him like he's already in the grave. The old man gives them a spicy earful about doors and windows. I'm guessing he's crazy. He unpacks a full cuss-out, and after they leave, he keeps cussing. The bandage on his head has blood. Something about him looks friendly, but I don't know any old batos, so I don't linger on it.

I think about the badass gringo, who is another kind of crazy that's more like a cornered dog — one that fights instead of runs. How he left me painted into a cop-killing corner makes me think that Zuky is right about calling me a dumbass. A shot dumbass. My foot hurts bad.

"WHERE TO?" Magaña asked.

"El Carrizo."

"The town?"

"Yes."

Rugg watched him weigh the news.

"Are you sure? It's a craphole."

"You said it, Commander. Where rats go."

They left the city and retook the highway with the bagged money in the Acura's trunk.

On Rugg's mobile another missed call from Sue, followed by a fusillade of inquisitional texts. *Why don't you answer? Do you have Rose? Should I come?* He laid the phone on the seat. From the consulate no missed calls. Eric White on to another crisis, Rugg guessed. Or diplomatic housework. When Rose was in the car, he would call him.

He checked his watch, recalling the departure time seen at the Los Mochis airport. Today's flight to Hermosillo departed; Rugg with the dead certainty that tomorrow's flight not one he should wait for. Another night spent here the same as bad luck pushed too far. "Is there an airport in Navojoa?" he asked.

"Not much of one," the commander answered.

"What does that mean?"

The commander said the Navojoa airport had no scheduled flights. "Only private planes use it."

"Are there soldiers?"

"Soldiers are at every airport. It is what they watch. You are a pilot. You know the business of some planes."

Rugg took in the overcast sky and the distant precipitation shafts that slanted darkly through the grayness. To the north the horizon towered with flat-topped, cumulus anvils. He removed his cap and dropped it on the front seat. He told the commander to wear it. "You better hope none of your patrol pals recognize you. That will end it."

They crossed the Río Fuerte bridge and paid the toll at the San Miguel plaza. In the Barobampo hills Rugg waited until the highway saddled into a straightaway before he instructed the commander to pull into the breakdown lane and put the Acura in Park.

"Why here, Mr. Rugg?"

"Do it!"

After they stopped, he took the duct tape from the floor and tossed it on Magaña's lap, telling him to tape his left wrist to the steering wheel at the ten o'clock position.

"What?"

"Don't go deaf on me." Rugg repeated the instructions. When the commander said he was left-handed, Rugg said, "I know." He watched Magaña use his right hand to wrap the tape over his wrist and under the steering ring. "More," Rugg said, checking the straightaway for traffic. "Speed it up." The commander wound the tape until Rugg told him to tear it with his teeth and leave the roll on the passenger seat.

"Is this necessary? I have fully cooperated."

"Keep it that way."

Rugg did not want Magaña abandoning the car should he need to get down for Rose. He did not tell the commander that the plan had changed, that they would not be returning to Los Mochis but would drive Rose in the Acura to the consulate in Hermosillo.

"How am I supposed to steer?

"With your life, Commander."

His right hand held tightly to the wheel as they retook the highway. Rugg reached forward to retrieve the tape. He bit off a short length, which he stuck on the seatback in front of him. "Speed limit," he said.

They drove. Rugg removed the stripper clip affixed to his abdomen and detached the cartridges from the clip, dropping them into the cupwells. He took some of the cartridges and buttoned them inside his shirt pocket, where he kept Rose's picture. The stripper clip on his ankle he left in place. He took the commander's compact from his pocket and flicked off the safety, setting the pistol back in the grip well on the passenger door.

Ahead, the highway embayed by dark, low-slung clouds. The first large drops pancaked the windshield. Rugg gazed at the glass. Weeks stranded here and not once had it rained. He wondered what could go right of all the possible outcomes to go wrong that would bring a sudden and crashing end to his chances. Rain likely not one of them.

Rugg saw no advantage in his corner. Not the guns, not the place, not the legs. No control. His cause with warrant but without deputy. In the other man's corner, everything — a thirteen-year-old girl worth nothing to him. The money not a premium and not even a ransom. *I do not need your money as much as you need your daughter.* In such a bargain, no greater advantage than needlessness.

He knew she might not be there, that they might shoot him on sight. He knew that no plan survives the first contact with an enemy. He knew that good intentions sometimes fall short for no reason other than that good intentions are not enough to prevail. Sometimes evil has a better plan. Sometimes luck rides the worst horse. He had flown and he had fallen from flight, and there was no right of survival connecting the two. He had shot and killed men while they had shot back and not killed him, their bullets taking different paths. He considered himself better prepared than most men for the onslaught of chance and its improbable outcomes. But he also wondered how many deaths a man could outlive before fortune favored him no longer. One more would be enough, he hoped. One. To bring her home.

Rain descended on the Acura, the windshield awash in cinereal silver, the highway eclipsed. "Chingado," blurted the commander. He took his free hand off the wheel to move the wiper lever on the column, steering with his taped wrist. "I need both hands," he complained.

"No, you don't," Rugg said.

They drove, the rain pounding the car, a black sky pressed upon them. Rugg watched him, how he clung to staying alive. "Lights," he said.

Again, Magaña took his hand off the wheel. The Acura swerved. "You want to get us killed, Mr. Rugg?"

They pushed through the downpour, the car buffeted by the storm's gust front, the commander gripping the wheel, his knuckles white. After the rain, a sudden quiet.

"I thought you are not afraid to die," Rugg said.

The commander said he was no coward. He simply did not wish to die foolishly, and for nothing.

Rugg reminded him of what he had said about luck playing largely in their lives and deaths. "If you were to die on this highway driving one-handed in a hard rain, your death would be no less foolish than if you were killed by a man shooting you in the back. Your death would be for nothing and no different than the death of the man who pointed the HK rifle at your head before the follower jammed to save your corrupt ass."

The commander said he had exaggerated about the weapon jamming.

"Ah," Rugg said. "Then maybe I will test this one."

They drove. Magaña said he had done everything asked of him. "Why shoot me? I'm helping you to find your daughter."

Rugg counted the rounds in the cupwells. "Because you did not protect her."

"I don't understand."

"I know."

"How could I protect your daughter? I don't patrol the highway."

"But you did once. You had your chance to protect. Now the men who work for you have their chance. Men like Tomás. They follow your lead and serve these fiends who took my daughter."

The commander looked at Rugg in the rearview. "I am not to blame for what happened to you and your daughter."

Rugg laid the Smith & Wesson on the seat before he detached the length of tape stuck to the seatback. He leaned forward and clapped the tape over Magaña's mouth and pressed it to the sides of his jaw. "Time for you to shut up."

When the commander lifted his driving hand to remove it, Rugg retook the pistol and rapped the barrel on his head. "Don't. Just drive."

The commander's muffled protests spilled into his eyes.

"Breath and listen. Mostly listen. You may live."

They drove, the rain pounding again, the world beyond unseen. Rugg opened the flip phone and read the time stamp on the gavillero's call. Two hours gone, the afternoon all but spent. Dusk to descend early on the clouded land, and he did not want to be found here with her after dark. He pulled the Colt pistol from the seat pocket and set it beside him.

The rain broke, and Rugg glimpsed the highway sign. Ahead, he saw the flat-laid town of El Carrizo spread to fallow fields, an unfinished church steeple the tallest structure. "Slow down," he said.

At the highway turnoff stood a one-island Pemex station besieged by a clutter of tarpaulined eating stands and wheeled food carts. Rugg observed the vehicles parked off the highway and those idling near the entrance. He knew any one of them could have a lookout.

They entered the town through a masonry archway built with clearance for stakebed trucks and cattle racks. The main street laid with concrete adoquín. The unpaved side streets narrow and mud-rutted. When Rugg told the commander to find the church, they drove to the town plaza — an unkempt and grassless square of ground crisscrossed by the compacted footpaths of men. On the plaza stood the church. Rugg instructed Magaña to turn the block and drive to the next street.

The alley behind the church pooled with rainwater in the tracks and bajos. They drove slowly, the Acura bottoming in the mud. Rugg watched for a white house with a gate. At the end of the alley they reversed on a cross street before doubling back behind the church in the opposite direction. Then Rugg saw it.

The house built back from the alley near the end of the block. The paint once white, the gate chained. Tire tracks rutted the front yard, but no vehicles sat outside the house.

"Don't stop," Rugg said. He glanced behind them before they turned the corner and drove to the plaza, where he told Magaña to loop a backtrack.

On the second pass they stopped at the gate. "Keep it running," Rugg said. He observed the tire tracks sunk in the mud. Wide treads left by trucks or big passenger vehicles. The yard littered with empty bottles and disposable plates. Rugg took in the house. The windows covered with aluminum foil. The front door made from welded steel panels. Above the door hung a porcelain lamp socket with an incandescent bulb. The light on.

Rugg lowered his glass. The pistol he held below his chest should he need to shoot out the window. When the commander saw him, his taped lips rippled with grunted queries. Rugg told him to shut up.

Outside, the damp air hung with woodsmoke wafted from neighborhood cookfires. Rugg sniffed. A good smell that belonged somewhere else, somewhere safe. He checked his watch. The hour later than the appointed time. He had hoped for a swift exchange with minimal parley, the money worked out between villains once Rose was in the car. No hope too small to sustain.

He surveyed the alley, and then he took in the fenceline to the corner of the lot, where a concrete electric pole stood with the aerial feed for the house. The base of the pole mounted with a breaker box and a utility meter. Rugg told Magaña to reverse the Acura and put him even with the pole. From the window he regarded the meter, watching the rotation of the aluminum disk. Something more than a lightbulb drew power. He reached out and tripped the breaker, the door light turning off.

They waited. The house without movement. He checked behind them. No vehicle approached. The alley made for an ambush, he told himself. Their exit easily boxed at either end. If the Acura hung in the mud, they were ducks. He opened the flip phone and spiked the volume before he called, letting it ring. He watched the house.

The sonofabitch.

He knew better than to get down. "Vamos," he told the commander.

After the Acura retook the adoquín street, he called again, listening. He closed the phone and observed the vehicles that passed them; no Cherokee spotted. When they reached the highway, he told the commander to double back to the main street. Rugg looked behind them. He called again. After he closed the phone, he set it on the seat.

They parked off the street, a light rain falling, dusk unfolded from the clouded sky, the town cast to grayness. Rugg stared out the window. He thought of his dead wife and how she had loved to walk in the rain, and what she would say if she saw him in this place, the world mired in mud, and he a blind man in search of their only child. His promise to keep their daughter safe an empty assurance, one that profaned her last breath and mocked his vigilance. The idea to bring Rose here had been his, and then he had brought her, and here he was without her, and nothing would be the same again. The daughter he found would not be the one he lost — not the child, not the shadow of the child, not the shadow's memory of itself — and where would that leave them? Beyond words. Beyond silent recrimination. His truancy willfully ventured, her life gambled for nothing. What left for him now was to save her until he could not.

Magaña pointed to his taped mouth.

"No," Rugg said.

He tipped an imaginary bottle to his lips.

"No."

The rain let up. Daylight an ashen trace. He retook the phone and called, and then he told the commander to return to the church. In the alley they found the ruts topped with water, no ridge shadows to guide them. When the commander reached to turn on the headlights, Rugg told him to run dark. "Don't stop and don't get us stuck or we both die."

The commander proved a practiced operator in mud not of his own making. When the Acura hung, he maintained momentum, allowing the tires to spin but not trench. They fishtailed down the alley. When they passed the house, Rugg saw no vehicles. The light above the door still dark.

"Drive," he said.

He called the number again, listening. The phone battery almost drained.

The sonofabitch.

They idled off the highway near the Pemex station. Nearby, the tarpaulined eating stands lit with strings of colored bulbs. Rugg saw rowed customers hunched over their steaming plates. How men ignored extremities that were not their own. Each life a mystery to all others, and then a mystery to none.

When Commander Magaña pointed to the fuel gauge, Rugg ignored him. He sat silent and gutted, no sense made of it. If they held Rose — or if they didn't — why hadn't they intercepted him at the house? To ambush or to overpower, if nothing else. Their method beyond his understanding. Or a method not meant for reason, like the perverse causes sprung from a place where the planet gyred backward, and men faced west for daybreak and hope.

What now?

He observed a cabover truck taking on diesel at the pump island, and he watched the boy who climbed onto the truck and how he hung precariously from the cab roof to wash the glass. Nothing safe, Rugg told himself. None of it and no one, and so the world.

He looked over the commander's shoulder to read the fuel gauge before he instructed him to retake the highway south.

The day's remains fled. The hour without traffic. Beyond the highway the desert swept of shapes and shadows. Rugg took the folded picture from his shirt pocket. He opened it and stared at her face in the dim light. No memory of Rose the same since. Even the clearest blurred by her absence. A ruination of remembrance that tore at his heart and left him sick and desolate, his anger fed. He laid the picture unfolded on the seat beside him. The asphalt tire drone loud in his head. No need to check his watch to know that time kept no hostage. Soon the dead cop would catch up. The live one not to be leashed another night. One leg to outrun it all, and how to find her if they did not find him first.

They had passed the turnoff to Poblado Cinco when headlights rose onto the highway behind them. A blue flasher lit, the Acura's interior cast with its sapphire iteration. In the mirror Rugg saw two vehicles close on them. No sirens sounded.

"Yours?" he asked.

Commander Magaña looked to the rearview and shook his head. His eyes large. Rugg put the Colt between his legs and flicked the safety off the Smith & Wesson. He set his right hand on the grip well of the door, where he had laid the compact pistol. "High beams," he said. "Stay left. Make ready to brake." The commander switched lanes. The median strip a grassed gully. Rugg watched for the first crossover to the northbound lanes. When he spotted it, he told Magaña to turn. The crossover wide but not graded. The Acura dropped off the asphalt and chopped roughly across puddled ruts and chuckholes. When it stopped, Rugg ordered Magaña to back up. The commander fumbled with the shift lever before they reversed, the Acura coming around. Rugg heard the cop's muffled curses, and then he heard them articulated when the commander tore the tape from his mouth. "¡Qué chingados. Nos van a matar!"

Rugg struck him with the pistol and told him to shut up. The commander tugged and twisted his taped wrist to free himself from the wheel. "¡Pinche gringo loco!" Rugg hit him again. "Cálmese," he said before he reached forward and knocked the sun visors from their brackets and swatted them vertical. He sat back and lowered his window, positioning the pistol inside the door post. "Agacharse," he said.

The commander ducked.

The lead vehicle with the flasher. When it entered the crossover, the Acura's high beams made the driver and the front-seat passenger raise their arms. Their faces masked, the one riding shotgun showing a raised pistol, his intention manifest. Rugg hesitated, reading the cab's interior as the vehicle skidded, his best guess the near certainty that Rose not in the lead car. He shot the driver first, and then he shot the pistol bearer, both in the chest with sequenced rounds, their heads thrust forward from the impact. The truck a white pickup with an extended cab. Rugg saw other passengers piled in the rear seat. He watched the pickup careen and circle out of the crossover and into the grassed gully, where it rolled on its side and stopped with the cab pitched nose up, no dust raised in the wet grass. He heard the cries and shouts of the occupants. The commander swore. Rugg eyed the truck's silhouette and he shot the first figure who climbed from the cab's broke-out glass, dropping him onto those inside.

The second vehicle the black Cherokee, the sun visors down when it entered the crossover and swerved broadside before Rugg dared a high shot at the driver. In the headlight glare he glimpsed the silver hair of the front-seat passenger, no mask on his face. Rugg slid behind the commander, but he did not shoot. The Cherokee with its windows up, the tinted glass reflecting the Acura's headlights. He knew that if she was inside, she was in the rear.

An automatic weapon fired from the rolled pickup, the rounds spitting the puddled water, the gun flash from a weapon periscoped out the window by a raised arm. Rugg shot into the pickup cab until the flashes stopped, and then he dropped the empty magazine and waited for a chance to reload from the cupwells. He took the Colt and flicked off the safety. The commander raised his head high enough to bite the duct tape that held his wrist. His free hand tried to unwrap it. Rugg hit him. "You're dead if you go. I'll shoot you first." Magaña swore and called him a gringo fool. When Rugg looked at the Cherokee, he saw it sway as the gavilleros offloaded from the backside. The Acura headlights illuminated the footwork of their deployment to the front and rear of the vehicle.

Rugg knew they outgunned him: why he had fired first. Not for the odds but for the gamble that they would kill him where he sat, take the money, give nothing. But would they kill a Federal Police commander?

No sounds reached him from the rolled pickup. No cars passed on the highway. The Acura idled. Rugg watched the Cherokee. He told the commander to lower his window and identify himself.

Magaña used his free hand to toggle the switch. He called out. "¡No disparen! Soy el comandante de la Policia Federal."

Someone guffawed. In the headlight wash Rugg saw the Cherokee's front passenger window open partway. He recognized the graveled voice that ordered the commander to get down with his hands raised.

"No puedo," Magaña protested. He said he was taped to the wheel.

The boss lowered the window. Rugg saw him the same as he remembered. The short-cropped silver hair. The handsome face beyond good looks.

"Who is this man commanding?" he asked in English.

Rugg offered no reply. Magaña called out that the gringo had money in the trunk. He said he was willing to make a satisfactory arrangement.

El Sin spat out the window. Rugg saw their gun barrels laid flat on Cherokee's hood. He lifted his voice. "Where is she?"

When he heard no answer, he asked again.

The reply came. "She's not here."

"You said you had her."

"I did. Now I don't."

Rugg called out her name to no answer. El Sin looked to where the pickup had crashed. "You cost me a new truck."

"You lied."

"I did. In Mexico, we believe many lies because we tell many. I think you are becoming Mexican."

"Where is she?"

"I told you. Not here."

Rugged called her name again. He waited. "You sonofabitch. I did what you said."

"And I told you. A man's word is worth nothing. We do not live in the good old days, as you gringos call them."

Rugg observed a gavillero break from the cover of the Cherokee into the grass behind the crossover and out of the light. Too quick for a shot.

El Sin addressed the commander. "Apaga las luces, comandante."

Rugg told Magaña not to touch the headlights.

The commander didn't move.

"It would be a shame to shoot them," El Sin said.

"Shoot them," Rugg countered.

"The commander has a nice car. Before all else, I am a car thief."

"Before all else, you are a predator of children," Rugg shouted. "Scum." He kept the crossover in view, the Colt sighted distantly. The lone gavillero would traverse the clearing to get behind them.

"I did not touch your daughter, gringo. It is not my habit."

Rugg said he didn't care about his habits. "Where is she?"

"She is where she is."

"Cut the bullshit."

"It is not easy to know what to do, gringo."

"Where is she?"

"I told you. Gone."

"Where?"

"Far from here. You were right, what you said that day, that she is more trouble than you. Maybe she is trouble enough to survive. But you are still the ugly one."

"You'll be the ugly one soon enough if you don't give me my daughter. Where is she?"

Rugg heard his graveled voice speaking to others.

"Where is she?"

"Making new friends. You will not see her again. The time to accept this has caught up with you."

Rugg did not let this man's verdict diminish the truth spoken: she was alive, she was trouble. Like her old man. His Rose. "I will give you the location of the boy, your scout," he offered. "A trade. Location for location."

El Sin laughed. "I have already traded for his whereabouts at a cheaper price. Maybe you should have killed him. Maybe you should have left his phone where you killed him. But you did neither. So, here we sit. And he lies in the hospital. When we finish with you, we will visit him. Did you bring my Colt?"

Rugg looked to the crossover, the dim-lit gap. He knew the target would look black when it broke.

"We can deal," he said. "The commander is in your debt. There is twenty thousand dollars. Let me go. If she is far from here, as you say, you will not be troubled. I will become another man's problem."

The boss laughed again. "The last time I gave you the chance to run, you came back. I do not think you can run so well now. My chances of guaranteeing that I don't see you again are better this time."

Magaña twisted his taped wrist. He urged Rugg to release him. He promised to negotiate their safe passage from this desperate jam. He said these highway thugs would listen to him. Rugg told him to stay still and shut up. He looked to the crossover. "Do we have a deal?" he called to the boss.

"You have nothing to deal, gringo."

"I do. I have the commander. If I kill him, the mess will fall to you. It will follow you and your men. His death will come before mine, and then yours will come once they hunt you down. Tell me where to find my girl. Let me live. Save yourself from the mess of a dead commander. Put him in your pocket instead."

When Rugg saw the shadowed shape of the lone gavillero dart into the gap, he lifted the Colt slightly and shot a succession of rounds, leading with each. He saw the figure stumble and pitch headlong into the grass.

He looked to the Cherokee. "Send another and I'll do him too," he shouted. He reached to the cupwell to reload the Smith & Wesson. Then the Acura's dome lamp lit, and the driver's door opened. Rugg saw Magaña lunge from his seat.

"¡No disparen!" the commander shouted to the gavilleros. "Soy el comandante."

He stood with raised hands, his pants pressed to his buttocks from the hours seated. Torn duct tape clung to his wrist.

Last card, Rugg told himself.

The commander announced that the gringo carried three pistols, that he could be killed once his ammunition was spent.

El Sin watched from his window. "Bien," he replied. He told Magaña to step away from the car.

The Acura door left open. Rugg broke the dome lamp with the pistol.

The commander lowered his hands and advanced toward the Cherokee. On his head rode Rugg's green mesh cap.

The first shot stopped him, as though he had walked into a roofbeam chin-high. The mesh cap flew off his head together with his scalp, the commander falling in a lump. The shots that followed made his lifeless body jitter and jump.

Rugg stared, his shot at Magaña's back still chambered in the Colt. When he looked to the Cherokee, he saw the boss pointing a pistol one-handed out the window. The weapon silver, like his hair. In the loud quiet El Sin said, "I don't need a commander in my pocket when I have his boss next to my balls."

His pistol raised where Rugg could see it. When he opened the Cherokee door and stepped down, Rugg aimed the Colt at his chest. Then a shape blocked his view, and the lone gavillero who had run the crossover stood in the window. He struck Rugg's hand, knocking the Colt away, the sound of a puddle splash what Rugg heard before the gavillero grabbed him by the hair and yanked his head out the window.

"Roon, greengo," he slurred.

The smell of grass strong on him. In the wash of reflected headlights, Rugg saw the knife, its glint and unsheathed length, the suspended motion and how it would arc to the first slash. He reached beneath him, his hand searching for the grip well in the door handle where he had laid the compact pistol. He grasped it, the tight-handed fit. The gavillero bettered his grip on Rugg's hair and pulled his head down, pressing his neck on the window channel. Rugg hooked the compact above him and fired blindly, the shots close to his ear. The weight on him lifted, his hair relinquished, the gavillero falling backward, his shadow, his grassed smell. Rugg lowered the pistol and shot him repeatedly, his unmasked face white in the darkness, his mouth a black hole.

Rounds wasted, Rugg thought.

When he looked up, El Sin stood beside the Acura, his silver pistol pointed. Behind him stood another gavillero wearing a mask with painted horns and teeth. The gun he held not aimed at Rugg but at the boss's back.

Rugg raised the compact and squeezed the trigger.

Then the headlights went out.

20

In the morning Dr. Sanchez comes to check the batos bed by bed. When he gets to mine, he says he's happy to see me. His thin mustache makes him look happy. He asks how my foot feels, and I answer that it feels ready for walking, which is a lie. He tells me that I need to practice on crutches first. He says that as soon as a pair become available, the nurse will bring them. I hope soon is pronto because the ministerial cop promised to see me soon. Crutches could change that. The gringo shot me from crutches, so I'm not discounting their value. First, I need clothes.

The doctor doesn't unbandage my foot, but he makes me wiggle my toes, and then he sticks the underside with something sharp he took from his pocket. I don't expect it, and I jerk my foot away. "Mucho mejor," he says, though I don't feel any better after he does it. He calls me a lucky boy and starts the old story about the Program of Attention to Adolescents at Risk and how he is going to speak to the authorities about my positive attitude. I don't tell him that attitude is what got me shot. Instead, I tell him that the police came and left, but the pain in my foot hangs around, asking for pills. He smiles and promises to investigate — an answer that sounds low on likely.

He's still standing by my bed when the first shots crack the hospital quiet. The shots make him jump. In the next bed the old man suddenly comes alive. "¡Otra vez!" he cries, as though he knows its trouble. Shouts come from the hall. A woman screams. I see the cop get up from his chair by the door. He reaches for his holster, and that's the last thing he does on his feet. Two shots blow him backward, where he flops to the floor and doesn't move. They come through the door the way the Indians pile into the prairie houses in the Old West movies. When I see the masks, I feel a heavy stone fall on me. I try to get up, but I can't. I know they'll give it to me point blank. The old man shouts something about how the devil shot him. He rolls off his bed — I hear him hit the floor — then he doesn't speak. There's more shooting in the hall, and I recognize Zuky from his mask with the painted horns and the grinning teeth. He comes toward me. The heavy stone sinks me so far into the bed that I feel like I'm disappearing. My voice won't come out. I think, "This is it, this is when cowards get remembered."

Dr. Sanchez doesn't move from my bedside. When Zuky orders him to scram, the doc steps between me and him. He identifies himself as a doctor. Maybe he thinks a man wearing a devil's mask and carrying a gun respects a doctor. He tells Zuky that he cannot stand by and allow harm to come to his patient. Zuky shoots the doc without raising the barrel of his AK. Doctor blood hits my face, and then Zuky rakes him with bullets after he falls, and there's no doc deader than Dr. Sanchez.

I don't see El Sin, but I know he always comes in at the end, like the Comanche chief holding back until it's time to cut out the hearts of the scalped losers. Then Zuky says, "Can you walk, dumbass?" I'm not expecting to hear dumbass again, or to hear anything again. I stare at his mask. His real teeth show. They grin like the painted ones. I shake my head, waiting for the joke to end. When I tell him I'm naked, he calls me a good-for-nothing queer, and then I know I'm OK. Fer comes up. I recognize his beard where the mask doesn't cover. Nacho stands beside him. He doesn't wear a mask, only a kerchief over his nose and mouth, like a bank robber. They carry me out in the bedsheet, and

I hear Zuky shooting his AK in the room. I don't know if he found the old man. We pass the screaming woman in the hall, and outside there's another cop down in his blood. At the curb our ride idles with Cachoro behind the wheel. I don't see El Sin. We take the highway, and Zuky rides shotgun. He says he won't call me Speedy anymore. It gets a laugh.

$\mathcal{T}$HE TRUCK TIRES whined on the asphalt.

The girls lay on the back seat of the club cab, their mouths taped, their hands and feet bound with nylon cable ties. They felt the vehicle drop off the asphalt and stop.

The second vehicle, a Ford Excursion, waited in the breakdown lane. Two men descended and came to the passenger door of the truck. They pulled the girls from the back seat, taking them by the legs. The girls kicked and twisted, their screams muffled. No cars passed on the highway. The driver of the Excursion got down to open the tailgate doors. After the men loaded the girls in the cargo space, they climbed into the Excursion without hurry. The club cab truck crossed the median strip and took the highway north. The Excursion drove south.

21

At the El Carrizo house they lay me on a mattress. Later they bring the town doctor who takes care of our crew. He gives me a shot and some pills for the pain, and he says the same thing the dead doc said about practicing with crutches before I can walk. I don't see El Sin, and I don't ask for him, but when the crew goes out, Perico tells me everything that happened after I called in the signal at the hotel — how they found the white Ranger parked on the street with no gringo inside it, and how they went into the hotel and found the room where he stayed, and how they shot an old man at the desk for pretending to know nothing, and shot up the hotel, and then how they looked for me, which caused an argument between Zuky and El Sin over whether I ran or got lifted by the gringo. Perico says he received orders to meet up that night, and he rode with El Sin, Zuky, Cachoro, and the crazy Güero in the Cherokee, while XL drove *the pickup with Niquelado, Tecolote, Chango, and the Mazatleco, all of them taking to the highway near Poblado Cinco, where they caught the gringo in an Acura with his driver, who was a cop, and not just any cop but a federal commander, which means the gringo wasn't lying about the bato. Perico says the gringo ambushed XL, making the pickup roll, none of the crew walking away, and then El Sin and the gringo faced off ride to ride while Güero del Café snuck around to kill him, getting killed himself, and finally, El Sin got down with Zuky from the Cherokee and he shot the gringo and the gringo shot him and Zuky fired too, and the only one who walked away was Zuky. There was a payout in the Acura's trunk they took before they burned the car with the gringo, the cop, and Güero del Café inside. The crew in the pickup were left for the funeral van to pick up and deliver to the families. El Sin was buried in the desert because Zuky didn't want the cops to know he was dead.*

That's what Perico tells me. "We crew for Zuky now," he says.

It's a heap of news piled on at once. There's no good way to hear about dead bodies — burned, buried, or delivered. What's the difference? If all dying is one flavor to the dead, then staying alive is all that's left to the rest of us. For me, shot and alive is better than shot and dead. I'll take it.

At least the gringo got what was overdue. The crazy Güero too. If there's a place where dead dogs go to bark, he's gone there. I figured El Sin was too scary to die early, but I was wrong. Maybe Zuky saw the future. He said I might work for him someday, and someday came. Maybe he's smarter than El Sin. I still wonder why he sprung me from the hospital, but I don't ask when I see him. I've heard dumbass enough already.

Zuky gives me the crutches that belonged to the gringo, and he orders Cachoro to shorten them to my size. He says that as soon as I can walk, we're driving to Culiacán where the gringo's blondie daughter was sold to a girlie joint. He says he will buy me a night with the gringa if I promise to shoot her in the face. Her sad face. He gives me the Colt.

AT THE LOS MOCHIS airport, the woman exited the gate and walked past the soldiers deployed in the terminal. She wore blue jeans and tennis shoes, and she carried a backpack. At the queued taxis she set down the pack and took from one of its pockets a folded paper. "Taxi, por favor," she told a driver. She read from the paper. "Hotel San Carlos."

The driver nodded. She did not let him take the pack.

In the taxi she stared at the cane fields as they drove to the city.

M. S. HOLM was born in Boston and raised in New England. He worked variously as a dishwasher, taxi driver, dockhand, and substitute teacher. He lives in Mexico.